# CHAPTEn 1

I can tell you how many shots it'll take before a bullet chamber is empty. I can tell you precisely where to shoot if you want to kill someone, maim them, or just graze them. I can tell you how to elicit the loudest screams when a person is tortured.

What I can't tell you is how it feels to love someone. What I can't tell you is how it feels to be alive.

———————

MY GAZE STRAYS down to the people kneeling at my feet. Two men, one woman. Their mouths are moving, and I know they're begging for mercy. But my brain has blocked out their cries. All I can hear is the roaring in my ears; all I can feel is the ice chilling my veins. My mind is miles away, pretending like I'm not even here. Like I don't exist.

I drift back to consciousness in time to hear the question directed at me.

"What do you plan to do with them?" one of the capos asks.

1

Michael Slade. He's been loyal to the family for years. My father saved him when he was a kid, pulled him from the streets, clothed him, fed him, and then sent him to school. He owes us everything.

For the longest time, I used to think true loyalty was earned. But loyalty comes at a price. Sometimes the price ranges, it differs, but ultimately, you can't earn anything without giving something in return. That's just how life is.

The only thing you earn for free is your family. People like Michael Slade are loyal because their conscience drives them to be.

Conscience—another thing that feels foreign to me. I haven't had a conscience in years.

"The Don's orders were clear," I say, glancing at Slade's focused blue eyes. "Kill them."

When Slade hesitates, I grab my gun and point it at the woman's head. Mentally, I recite all I know about her.

Clara Jane, 28 years old. She joined the D'Angelos last year, seeking a break. She agreed to deal drugs for us as a side job. Things were going well. Until she got sloppy, messed up, and tipped off the police that she was a drug pusher for us. In a bid to escape jail, she flushed her supply down the drain.

It would have been fine if she'd stopped there. Losing the drugs was stupid but we would have forgiven her. But then Clara approached a rival gang and offered to trade the family's secrets in order to pay back her debt to us.

It was a betrayal. And it's unacceptable.

"Please," she cries, tears streaming down her face. "I have a little sister."

"She'll be taken care of" is all I say—right before a bullet hits the middle of her head.

# Contract With the Mafia Boss

**ASHLIE SILAS**

Clara falls to the ground. Her death quiets her accomplices, who stare with wide eyes, unbelieving and terrified.

With gritted teeth, I turn back to Slade. "Are you going to handle them, or should I?"

His throat bobs. He looks at me and nods his head. "I've got it, boss."

My jaw ticks as I walk out of the warehouse. I glance back at Clara's body, wishing I could feel something, anything. But all I feel is ice.

By the time I reach my car, there have been two more gunshots in quick succession. The entire ride to Christian's house, my mind is blank. I arrive at the gate and it's immediately opened, granting me access to the mansion.

Every time I drive onto the grounds, I remember a time when I was normal. A little kid with no worries and fears, innocent and so full of life. Then I almost died and everything changed. The events of one night made me the man I am today.

The house is quiet as I make my way up the stairs. Usually, the kids are running around, raising hell. Wondering where they are, I arrive in front of Christian's home office. One short knock and I hear my brother's voice asking me to come in. He's seated in his chair and Daniella's leaning on the edge of the table in front of him.

Her cheeks are flushed and I don't even want to think about what they've been up to.

"Hey," I say, walking in.

"Carlo." Christian nods in acknowledgment.

"Hey, Lo," Daniella greets enthusiastically.

"Where are the kids?" I take a seat in front of the desk.

They both turn to me with eerily similar grins.

"We dumped them with Toph and Kat for the night. Or a

few nights, but they don't know that yet," Daniella informs me, mischief shining in her blue eyes.

I shrug. "Toph can handle them."

"How did it go?" Christian asks curiously.

"Fine."

Daniella rolls her eyes. "You can talk about it. Four years of marriage and you're still trying to keep things from me."

"Because it doesn't concern you, *tesoro*," Christian tells her, his voice silky smooth and soft in the way it only ever is with his wife.

Sometimes it's hard to think that he's still the same man I knew four years ago. He's changed so much, and in a good way. Every smile, every look at his wife humanizes him more, very much unlike how he used to be. I'm glad—one of us should be able to live with their soul intact. Christian's family saved him. Dany gave him a reason to live that wasn't tied to his responsibility to the family.

"Stop saying it doesn't concern me," Dany says, agitated. "I am your wife. It's as much my family business as it is yours."

"You have absolutely no business calling the family business your business," Christian retorts, his voice rising slightly.

Dany has always been the only person that could rile him up, make him lose his edge. His kids manage to do so on occasion, as well.

"That doesn't make any sense!"

I interrupt before the argument can progress. "Are we going to talk about the Bianchis or not?"

They both turn to me, and Daniella's eyes immediately brighten at a chance to be involved.

"The Bianchis? The family that owns at least a quarter of the buildings in Manhattan?" she asks.

Christian shoots me a scowl.

"We were going to have to tell her eventually. You're taking her to the anniversary party, right?"

"Still," Christian murmurs, turning to his wife, who is waiting to be brought into the conversation. He sighs. "We're going to the annual Bianchi party in three weeks."

"That sounds fun. Why are we going? You've never shown an interest before," she states.

"Mr. Bianchi and our father used to be close when he was alive. But after he died, I never really had any interest in keeping up the relationship."

"Until now," Daniella says, her blue eyes inquisitive. "You want something from him, don't you?"

I smile. Christian groans.

"More like need," he mutters.

"Our new base of operations," I tell her. "We need a building large enough to house the new casino we're planning to open, with a big enough basement where we could conduct our more… unsavory activities."

Daniella rolls her eyes. "And Bianchi has that?"

Christian replies, "Like you said, he controls a quarter of the buildings in Manhattan. He has a building in Bayside that would be ideal for what we've got planned, in a neighborhood that would bring in a lot of traffic."

"If he was close to your dad, he should be willing to sell the building to you, right?"

"One would think," Christian says darkly.

"We met up with Bianchi a week ago and asked to buy it. But the old man's dead set on giving the building to his future son-in-law, instead. According to him, the building has a lot of sentimental value."

"Who's his future son-in-law?"

"He doesn't have one," I say. "He has one daughter and

she's single as far as I can tell. Which is why it's pretty annoying that he's holding out on something so lucrative for a son-in-law who doesn't exist yet."

"It's not like you can force him to give you the building," Daniella points out.

Christian and I exchange sinister smiles.

"We can damn well try."

One thing about D'Angelos is that we never quit. If we want something, we go at it with everything we've got until we get it. We're stubborn like that.

I have a vested interest in making sure this deal goes well. I was the one who suggested we purchase the building. Which means it's on me to take care of things. My brother trusts my judgment and I've never once let him down.

No matter what I have to do, we're getting that fucking building.

Daniella looks from me to her husband and sighs softly. "I guess we're going to a party, then."

---

CARA'S SCREAMS go quiet as I finish. Neither she nor I say a word as I fall down to the bed beside her, both of us breathing too heavily and still basking in the cathartic bliss.

Fuck, I love sex. The only thing that ever makes me feel deeply is sex. Granted, those feelings are temporary and it eventually subsides, but it's nice to have it as a release when things get too dark.

I force myself not to flinch when Cara places a kiss on the side of my face. I keep my gaze trained on the ceiling as she gets to her feet, pulling the blanket over her body.

"I'm going to go take a shower," she informs me.

She doesn't wait for me to acknowledge her words before

she heads into the bathroom. The sound of the shower running fills the hotel room.

I'm still in the same place when she steps back out. Without a word, she begins to put on her clothes.

"Carlo," she calls a few seconds later.

I finally look at her, finding her dressed and looking completely put together. Dark hair pulled up into a ponytail, every sign that she was just fucked wiped away.

"Yeah?"

She looks nervous. "I need a favor."

I stay quiet as I wait for her to tell me what the favor is.

"My mom's having a dinner in a few days. A few of our friends and family will be there. And I was wondering if you'd like to come."

She's not looking at me as she finishes her sentence. I sit up, resting against the headboard, and wait until her green eyes find mine.

"You asking me out on a date?"

Cara's beautiful and smart, and I like that she keeps me on my toes. She and I started this relationship—this arrangement a few years ago. We ran into each other and had sex, and the sex turned into a few weeks of casual dating. But I never let it go any further, and she ended it. Since then, it's been once-in-a-while encounters and I never thought it was anything more.

I thought she knew there were lines that couldn't be crossed.

"You're giving me those icy killer eyes," she mutters.

I manage a smile. "You know I can't."

She sighs. And to my surprise, she doesn't even push. "I know. But it was worth a shot."

"What's going on?" I ask, a little concerned.

She's one of the few people apart from my family that I actually give a shit about. She works for my brother, who owns an auto repair shop. And while sometimes the lines have been 'blurred, this is the first time she's ever tried to take things further.

"Nothing. I guess I've just been a little on edge lately. My dad's going to be released in a couple of weeks and I'm nervous, I guess."

I don't stand to comfort her, but I do offer words of encouragement. "I'm sure he'll be happy to see you."

"Yeah, but what if he's changed? What if I've changed? What if I'm not—"

I stop her tirade before it gets out of control. "He's your father. Family's always and forever."

I might not be sure about a lot of things, but I do know that. Cara nods, giving me a grateful smile.

"I need to go," she informs me.

"Okay."

She makes a move for the door but I stop her by calling her name. She doesn't turn around and I know she knows what I'm going to say.

"This thing between us was fun while it lasted, Car. But it's reached an end, okay?"

She still doesn't turn to look at me. "You're an asshole, D'Angelo."

"I know."

She walks out of the hotel room and I allow myself a few more minutes of solitary bliss before taking a shower myself and heading out. And right on time, too, because I receive a text from Christian asking me to come to the casino.

He probably wants to talk about our game plan for the Bianchi party. It's still weeks away, but Christian's nothing if not thorough.

# CHAPTER 2

*Tori*

"Tell me when it hurts, baby girl," I say softly, placing my gloved hands on her stomach.

The girl in front of me is nine years old. Her lower abdomen is slightly swollen and she flinches when I press down on it slightly.

"Ah," she cries softly, her green eyes welling with tears.

"It's okay, sweetie. I'll do my best to make you feel better. What's your name?" I ask. I press down on other areas of her stomach, but it seems the pains only limited to the swollen part of her abdomen.

"Sarah," she replies.

"Okay, Sarah. I'm just going to ask Mommy and Daddy some questions and run a couple of tests. After that, I'll know how to help make you feel better, okay?"

"You promise?"

My heart clenches as I stare at her. I reach over to smooth down some of her brown hair. "I promise."

She smiles when I wink. I get to my feet and move away from the hospital bed to talk to her concerned parents.

"How long has she been in pain?"

"A few days," the mother replies. I can see the fear clearly in her eyes, so much like her daughter's. "She complained a bit about her stomach when she got home from school and I didn't think much of it. I gave her some ibuprofen and the pain went away. Then, three days later, I noticed the swelling. I took her to a clinic and some drugs were prescribed. I thought she would get better, but then "

The mom pauses, too upset to continue.

"She was having some trouble using the restroom and I noticed some blood in her stool. I don't think it's happened before. I asked her and she said no but I didn't get an ounce of sleep after that." "And the pain got worse overnight. Which is when we brought her here," her dad finishes, his voice hard and firm.

I nod, chewing the side of my lip as I try to understand what I'm dealing with. "Any other symptoms I should know about?"

"Upset stomach and loss of appetite," her mom replies. "She hasn't been eating well."

"Any vomiting?" I question.

The woman shakes her head. "She did have to the potty several times and was very uncomfortable when she did."

"Does she eat a lot of greasy food?"

The parents exchange glances, their eyes wide. Her mom offers me a jerky nod.

"We own a fast-food restaurant."

"Gotcha."

"What's wrong with her?" the dad questions sharply.

"I can't say now, Mr. Kale. We'll have to run some tests to get a proper diagnosis but is there anything else you can think of that can help?"

They shook their heads. "Ok. Let me get to work on those tests so we can see what's going on. I'll ask the nurses to give her some medicine for the pain in the meantime. "

"But you have your suspicions. You can guess what's happening. You've seen something like this before, haven't you?" he presses.

"I would hate to give you a diagnosis without a proper examination and tests to go by. Especially since you guys have already been to a clinic for this same issue. I know you're concerned about your little girl, and I'll do my best to provide you with some peace of mind but for now, all I can ask is for you guys to be patient until we get the test results."

I can tell he wants to argue further but then he lets out a breath. He and his wife move to stand beside the hospital bed. One of the nurses approaches me.

"400 milligrams of acetaminophen and start up an IV," I inform her.

"You got it, Doc. Should I call Doctor Shatt down here?"

"No, we can call him after we've taken a blood test."

"Alright."

I order a battery of tests, including blood work, imaging, and an ultrasound. Sarah is brave through it all, holding onto her parents' hands as we proceed with the examinations.

While the team works on that, I head over to the front desk to fill in some paperwork. Thirty minutes later, I've got the results from the tests. I take one look at them and let out a soft breath. Instead of calling down my direct supervisor, I head to the fourth floor where his office is. After one quick knock, I step inside.

"Doctor Shatt?" I say, stepping toward his desk.

The middle-aged man raises his head to look at me. He nods once. "What do you need, Bianchi?"

I place the results in front of him. "A nine-year-old girl came in with a swollen abdomen."

"Symptoms?" he asks, looking through the results.

I tell him everything the parents told me. A frown pulls across his face.

"It's not what I think it is, is it?"

His expression is grim as he says, "If what you're thinking is gastric cancer, then yes, I think it's exactly that."

My heart clenches. "Fuck."

Dr. Shatt raises an eyebrow at my language. He's the head of the pediatric department, which consists of me, a second-year resident, and an attending physician. Sometimes I wonder why he chose to go into pediatrics since he can be a little rough around the edges, but he's a good man and I've seen how well he treats children. He's also a great doctor, and if he's confirming my diagnosis right now, then I can't keep my promise to that little girl.

"You should inform her parents so we can get her started on treatments," Shatt says to me, handing over the results.

I hesitate. "Could you please speak to them? You're much more, um… experienced."

He shoots me an unamused look. "We've had this conversation before, Bianchi. Relaying bad news is part of the job."

I chew the side of my lip, resisting the urge to bite my fingernails. I'm nervous. I can't think of anything but the faces of the little girl's parents as I tell them that their daughter has freaking cancer. I can only imagine the way the light will go out of their faces. How devastated they'll be.

"Please, sir. You'd explain it much better than me."

"The answer is no, Doctor Bianchi. Put on your big girl pants."

I sigh softly, an argument already locked and loaded, ready to go. But then he gives me that look, the one that dares me to question him, and I clamp my mouth shut. I have no choice but to go and deliver the news to the family. Whose lives are about to be changed forever.

After delivering the bad news to the Kales, I get to work on treating the little girl. Gastric cancer, or stomach cancer is a type of cancer that develops in the lining of the stomach. This cancer can occur in various parts of the stomach and may spread to other organs if not detected and treated early. Luckily, her cancer is in the early stages so we should be able to get her treated and she can return to her normal life. After starting up treatments for her, I finish up my rounds before heading home.

———

As soon as I drive on the grounds of our house, my eyes widen. There's a shiny new BMW with a red bow on top of it. One of the staff walks over as soon as I'm parked.

"Wellings, who owns that car?" I question curiously.

The man shrugs. "I don't know, miss, your father brought it in earlier."

"Dad's back from his trip?"

He nods and I grin. I haven't seen my dad in over a month. I quickly head inside while Wellings collects the keys so he can park my car in the garage. I find my parents in the living room watching a football game. My dad's yelling at the screen, cursing at the wide receiver for having terrible aim, when I clear my throat. They both turn to look at me and their eyes brighten.

My dad shoots to his feet and pulls me into a hug.

"There's my darling child," he says ostentatiously, kissing me on both cheeks.

I groan, despite the laugh that bubbles out of me. "Dad."

"What?" he questions. "Didn't you miss your old man?"

"Of course I did," I say, staring into his inquisitive brown eyes.

"Good because I missed you a lot, *mia cara*. How was work?"

"It was…" I sigh. "Work."

He hums like he understands, pulling me to sit beside him on the couch. I wedge in between him and my mother, who places her head on my shoulder. My family's love language is physical touch. And while usually I would indulge in a cuddle session with my parents, I'm pretty exhausted. My dad protests when I try to get up.

"No, we need to talk to you."

Those words are never followed by anything good.

"About?" I ask.

"Didn't you see your present?" Mom questions.

"My… present? Shit, you mean the car?"

She nods and I quickly turn to my father.

"It's for me?" I ask, eyes wide.

"Of course, sweetheart. I even had the inside remodeled to fit your tastes. You're long overdue for a new car."

Something about that sentence gives me pause, and it isn't the fact that he remodeled it. The car I'm driving right now was given to me for my birthday a year ago. It's not old, not by any stretch of the imagination. And while I'm immensely grateful, I can see the slight crack in my dad's expression that tells me something else is going on.

"You want something," I state.

My dad chuckles, smile lines pulling across his mouth. He's getting older, but my dad's always had a sort of youth-fulness to him that warms my heart. He might be in his sixties but the man could drop and do twenty push-ups right now. When I think about all he's done with his life, how hard he's worked to get here, I can't help but be proud of him. They're second-generation immigrants and he always used to tell me how hard life was for him as a kid. My grandfather worked hard to start the company and Dad has done his best to make it what it is today. Our lives are a far cry from how he grew up.

"Observant as always, my darling," Dad says with a chuckle.

My mom brushes her hand through my hair. "It's why we wanted to talk to you, honey."

"We think it's time you get married," my dad says quickly, sort of in a rip-the-Band-Aid-off kind of way.

My mouth drops. I quickly get to my feet from between them, placing my hands on my hips. "No."

"Yes," my mom retorts. "We've left you alone for long enough, Astoria."

"You're not getting any younger, *mia cara*."

"But," I splutter, "we had a deal."

"Yes, we did. We promised we'd wait until you completed your residency, but you've finished the first year, Tori. How much longer do you think we can wait? You're twenty-eight, and people in our circles are beginning to wonder."

"I don't care what they think," I snap.

"Well I do," my dad says firmly, his tone switching from "loving father" to "hardened businessman." "It's your responsibility to get married, Astoria, and to marry well."

My mom takes over, her voice still gentle. "We understand that you haven't had the time to date since you've been working so hard, which is why your father and I have a proposal."

I'm immediately wary. "You have someone in mind already?"

"Yes," my mom says brightly. "And it's someone you'll like. Dante Marino."

My cheeks heat. I may have confessed to having a school-girl crush on him when I was, like, thirteen, but it was nothing more than a passing phase. Obviously, my parents think me liking him more than a decade ago means I might still harbor some feelings for him now, which couldn't be farther from the truth. In fact, the last time I ran into him, I was pretty uncomfortable. I have zero feelings for him.

Their hearts are in the right place. From what I can tell about Dante, he seems like a good man on paper, making a name for himself managing his family's business. But that doesn't mean I want to marry him. Arranged marriages are common in our circles. I just thought I had more time.

"Mom, I-I can't," I say, my voice hoarse.

My dad's eyes narrow. "Why not?"

"Because," I flounder for a good excuse, "because I—"

Suddenly, my mom gasps. "Astoria. Is it possible you've met someone?"

The expression on her face is almost giddy, and my dad smiles at her insinuation. It's best to just go along with it, so I nod.

"Yes. Of course I've met someone."

"So you have a boyfriend?" Dad presses.

I've never been the best liar, but I do my best to sell it. "Sure. I am dating a man."

*Oh god. I'm so screwed.*

My dad's eyes narrow and he gets to his feet. "Alright, then. I expect you to bring your boyfriend to meet us next week."

My eyes bulge. "Next week?"

"Yes, darling. It's the company's anniversary party. I'd like to meet my future son-in-law there."

"Dad, I said I was dating him. The man hasn't gotten down on one knee yet."

Probably because he doesn't exist.

"Be that as it may, I'd like to meet him next week."

I swallow softly before nodding.

"Enjoy your new car, *mia cara*," he says, kissing my cheek.

My mom can barely keep still as she stands in front of me. I'm mere inches taller than her.

"Is he Italian?" she questions.

My mouth feels dry as I reply. "You'll find out at the party, Mother."

*We'll both find out.*

"Okay, then," she says. "I can't wait to meet him."

"Me too," I mutter quietly.

Then she's following my father out and I collapse back onto the couch. My mind whirs as I wonder where I'm going to find a boyfriend for hire.

I am so screwed.

---

## CARLO

All our plans have gone to shit, and it's all thanks to my youngest brother and his wife.

I grit my teeth as I take in everybody seated at the back of the limo. This party was meant to be about business, not a family event, but thirty minutes ago, we dropped my nieces and nephew at their grandmother's place. Topher and his wife, suddenly with a free schedule, opted to follow us, and so we all piled into the limo.

We were all invited to the party, but I'm uncomfortable with more than half of my family going to the same location. We didn't make any plans for protection.

"Oh, chill out, Lo," Toph murmurs, shooting me the mischievous grin that never strays too far from his face.

"Don't talk to me," I say, my jaw clenched.

"Are you upset that you're now the fifth wheel? Is that it?"

I swear I love my little brother, but sometimes I wonder just how well he'd be able to make taunting remarks if I shoved my fist through his jaw.

He must see something threatening in my expression because his smile slips. Topher turns to our other brother, who's quietly whispering something in his wife's ear.

"Why's he so mad?" he asks with a pout, pointing at me.

Christian looks up. He doesn't seem nearly as upset with our new stragglers as I am.

"Because you're party crashing?' Christian says like a question.

"But it's a Bianchi party," Toph points out. "I've been to more of those than everyone in this car combined. Salvador loves me."

That makes me perk up and I arch an eyebrow.

Daniella's the one to voice what I'm thinking. "He does?"

Toph nods. "Yeah. Plus, Kat's met him a couple of times as well. He's close with Jameson's father."

In the Upper East Side, everyone's connected to everyone, but Topher and his wife's presence might not be as much of an annoyance as I thought. I turn to my sister-in-law and shoot her a smile.

"How well do you know the Bianchis?" I ask her.

Katherine, who's currently in Topher's lap, pauses to consider the question.

"His daughter went to my high school, although she was a few years older than me and we barely spoke. But Toph's right, I've met Salvador. He likes me."

"The old man likes everybody," Christian states. "We need him to do us a favor and he's proving difficult."

Topher frowns. "Wait, you're attending this party to have a business meeting?"

I can't help a self-satisfied smirk. "Not feeling so good about crashing now, are you?"

He sighs. "Is it too late to ask you to drop us off at a club somewhere?"

Katherine slaps his chest. "I am not going clubbing. Don't be annoying." She turns to me. "What do you need help with?"

"You just might be my favorite sister-in-law, Kat," I tell her, grinning.

"Hey!" Daniella says, annoyed.

"Your time will come, Dany."

She huffs, leaning further into Christian's lap.

"Okay, everyone. Our mission today is to convince a very stubborn man to sell us a building," I announce.

Topher snorts. "You're doing all this for a building?"

"Shut up, *fratello*," Christian states, an edge to his voice, and Topher blissfully goes quiet.

"Everyone, turn up your charm."

Daniella grins. "You say that like you or Christian have any charms."

I let out a soft sigh. I love my family, but now I'm considering if this night will be even harder with their presence.

Christian can tell I'm getting frustrated. "We need tonight to go well," he says firmly.

"No matter what happens, we're not leaving that party until Bianchi agrees to sell to us."

Our plan fails. We arrived at the party to surprised glances from the other guests who've never seen so many D'Angelos gathered at one society function before. Apart from the ones hosted by us, of course.

The women quickly got on with socializing while me and my brothers kept a lookout for Bianchi. When he finally approached us, he was ecstatic, even hugging both Daniella and Katherine and congratulating them on joining our family. Things quickly went downhill when Topher tactlessly mentioned the building.

He's never had an affinity for business, but he can be a real idiot sometimes. Bianchi clammed up and left, telling us to enjoy the evening. Now, I'm smarting in front of the bar and wondering just how we'll be able to convince him to sell.

"Chill out, Carlo," Katherine says beside me.

"Your husband's an idiot," I retort, which causes her to smile.

"I know."

They got married just over a year ago, after the birth of their little boy. They worked through so many issues to get there, too—most of all, her parents' disapproval.

Katherine stays quiet beside me as we watch Topher talk to some of the guests, while Dany and Christian dance in the middle of the room. I might have been joking when I said Katherine's my favorite sister-in-law, but she's definitely the one I'm most comfortable with. We might have gotten off to a rough start, but we've come a long way. And I'm glad my brother has her. She's great at keeping him grounded.

"So what are we going to do about the building?" Katherine questions.

"Short of somehow becoming his son-in-law?" I say, gesturing at Bianchi. He's having a conversation with an elderly couple. When he chuckles, it reverberates across the room despite the soft music coming from the string quartet. "I honestly have no idea."

# CHAPTER 3

## *Tori*

I check my phone to see five missed calls from my dad and several texts from my mom asking where I am. I quickly reply to my mother, telling her I'm already here. I've been here for thirty minutes, in my beautiful, brand-new car, with fear slowly crawling up my veins.

It's highly likely I'll end the night engaged to Dante Marino.

It's not like I haven't tried to find a boyfriend. Apart from the severe lack of male friends willing to pretend to be in a relationship with me, I also tried to contact some agencies that take care of matters like this, but I decided against it at the last minute. My dad has a PI on speed dial. By the end of the night, he'd know everything about the man, including his occupation, and I'd be screwed. The one thing my parents despise is me lying to them.

For a second, I actually considered how they'd react if I showed up with one of my female friends instead. But the last thing my parents would believe is that I'm gay. I sigh, resting my head on the steering wheel. This is completely and utterly fruitless. I need to just walk in there and face the music.

The party's already in full swing. I'm two hours late and I'm sure my mom is fuming. I spot the pair of them in the center of the room and beeline away from there, heading to the bar instead. I order three shots of tequila. The bartender gives me an odd look, and I arch an eyebrow in reply. He places the drinks in front of me a few seconds later.

I don't hesitate before throwing back shot after shot. Once I'm done, I feel a presence at my back.

"Easy, love," someone chuckles.

I whirl around and come face to face with Dante Marino. Of course. He offers me a small smile as he stands beside me.

"Hi, Dante," I murmur.

"Hey, beautiful. You look amazing."

"Thank you," I say, glancing down at the magenta Armani dress.

It was the first thing I saw in my closet. I threw it on and applied some minimal makeup before making my way here. But with the way Dante's looking at me, one would think I'm as made up as a Victoria's Secret model. It's flattering but I'm uncomfortable with his presence.

It only confirms that my dad has every intention of moving forward with a marriage if I fail to turn up with a boyfriend. Which feels like a punch in my gut.

It's not like Dante's hideous or anything. He's pretty good-looking. Tanned skin, green eyes, and if I had to guess his height, I'd say he's at least 6'3". In another world, I'd be ecstatic to marry him. But I don't want to get married for the wrong reasons. And while Dante might act like a gentleman, something about him rubs me the wrong way. I just don't know what. And apart from that, I'm really not ready to commit to another person, marriage, or relationship-wise.

"How was London?" I ask the dark-haired millionaire.

He flashes a smile as he recounts his two-year trip to

Europe. He had been managing some of his family's subsidiaries but it was also a sort of vacation for him.

"That sounds wonderful," I say when he tells me about swimming with dolphins and his visit to Scotland. The tequila shots have finally caught up to me and before I can stop myself, I'm asking a question that should have never left my lips. "Just out of curiosity, what deal are you and my father brokering?"

He looks surprised and I know I should keep my mouth shut but the words are pouring out regardless. "I mean, there has to be something. Otherwise he would have never suggested a marriage."

Dante looks mildly amused, and a blush is starting to crawl up my cheeks. I have zero filter when I'm drunk.

"That's for me and your father to know, gorgeous. But it's nice to know you're seriously considering our future," he says, a smirk that I don't like on his face.

"I'm not seriously considering anything," I state.

He arches a confident eyebrow. "Oh really."

My gaze is pulled over to my parents, who are watching the two of us with pleased smiles. My heart clenches. "I need to use the restroom."

I don't wait for his reply before moving away from the bar. Several people try to stop me to talk, but I ignore them all in favor alleviating of the looming pressure in my chest. I have no idea how to stop this marriage but I can't myself with that guy.

Things get worse when I notice my mom approaching.

"Astoria," she calls.

"Oh shit," I mutter, rushing out of the ballroom.

I'm not watching where I'm going and before I know it, I'm colliding into someone's rock-hard chest. Whoever it is swears colorfully before reaching for my waist to hold me in place. I swallow as I slowly look up and my eyes meet dark brown ones. Everything slows to a stop as I stare at him. I'm not sure how much time passes—a few seconds, a minute. It seems like no time at all before he withdraws his arms from around me.

I stumble slightly before finding my balance.

Rude. But then my eyes stray to his face again. His hard expression, the way the muscles in his jaw tick. And how the obvious fury does nothing to dull his beautiful face. I blink once, twice.

"Watch where you're going," he snaps.

"A collision like that takes two people, genius," I snap back instinctively.

His eyes narrow. I take in his face again, wondering why he seems so familiar. Granted, I can't know everyone in attendance at the party, but there's something about him.

"Astoria!" my mom calls again and I whirl around to face her.

I laugh nervously, wobbling on my feet a little. *Sheesh, that tequila really got to me.*

"Hey, Mom," I greet, a little relieved my dad didn't follow her outside.

My mom's eyes study my face for a minute before moving to the man who's standing behind me. I can feel his presence like a vise around my heart.

"Mrs. Bianchi," he says coolly.

My eyes widen and I turn slightly to shoot him a confused look. *How the hell does he know my mom?*

"Carlo," my mom mutters.

*She knows him too?*

She's looking at me now and there's a strange expression on her face. One I decipher much too late.

"Astoria, is Carlo the man you wanted us to meet?" she asks.

Her expression is equal parts worry, equal parts excitement, and equal parts shock. Several milliseconds pass as I continue to stare at her, uncomprehending. The man behind me isn't saying a single word. Then, realization hits me like a bolt to my stomach as I finally understand what she's asking. My mouth falls open as I try to conjure an answer to her question.

Mom waits patiently while my brain threatens to self-combust. "Astoria?"

Again, I blame the alcohol in my system for the answer that's blurted out of my lips.

"Yes!"

I angle back toward the man and blink rapidly, trying to wordlessly confer a plea for him to go along with it. His expression is both curious and annoyed. It quickly turns to confusion when I place my hand around his arm.

"Mom, this is my boyfriend. Carlo," I announce with all the bravado I can muster.

Internally, I'm cringing and cursing myself. Of all the dumb things I've ever done, this might take the cake. The man, for his part, doesn't immediately wrench his arm away. But he does tense, and out of the corner of my eye, I see the sharp look he throws my way. I don't meet his gaze, I just continue to stare at my mother whose expression is one of complete surprise.

"You're dating Carlo D'Angelo?" she asks, her voice containing a note of wonder.

My eyes widen and I finally look up at him. That's why he was so familiar. He's a D'Angelo?

*Fuck my life.*

I don't know much about the family, but what I do know

is that they're dangerous and very familiar with a life of crime. Now I'm battling with the urge to drop my hand from his arm. My heart rate quickens as my mind finally catches up to the reality of my situation.

I remember Carlo now. He's not the most popular person in his family but certainly the most infamous. I've heard a lot of rumors. Of all the people I could have chosen to be my fake boyfriend.

"Yes, Mother," I reply, despite wanting nothing more than to swiftly deny and run far, far away. "I'm dating Carlo. Surprise?" I offer weakly.

She doesn't smile. She simply looks at Carlo.

"How did you two even meet? Why didn't you mention it when you were speaking to Salvador earlier? Why all the secrets?" she asks, seemingly affronted.

I open my mouth to reply but he beats me to it.

"I'm very sorry, Mrs. Bianchi. Your daughter and I wanted to keep our relationship secret for a while. You know how things are in our circles," he says. There's not a hint of deception in his voice. He even manages to sound sincere.

*He's going along with it?* I angle my head to read the expression on his face, but it's blank and dry. He appears unaffected by this whole ruse.

My mom is nodding in agreement. "I guess you're right. This is such good news."

One would think she'd be put off by the fact that her daughter is dating a member of a known crime syndicate, but from what I remember, my parents adore the D'Angelos. Something about their late father being a really good friend to Dad and helping him out when the company was in trouble.

"How long have you two been dating?"

"Mom," I say quickly, "why don't you head back into the ballroom and Carlo and I will join you soon? We have some things to discuss. He came to the party earlier than me and I haven't seen him all day. We have all the time in the world to talk later."

My mom smiles and after one last glance at us, she goes back inside—leaving me alone with a stranger who is apparently now my fake boyfriend. He doesn't even hesitate. As soon as she's gone, he rips his hand away and turns to me, dark eyebrows slightly raised in question.

"What the hell was that?"

# CHAPTER 4

## *Carlo*

M y jaw is tense as I stare down at the woman standing beside me. She shifts uneasily, her eyes darting around while she pointedly avoids eye contact.

The last few minutes have been nothing short of bizarre. I stepped outside the ballroom to grab something from the limo we brought and was returning only to run into her—literally. She made a nice indent on my chest before swaying on her feet, an action I'm going to guess was the result of inebriation. But not even that can explain what went down in the next couple of minutes.

"Well?" I ask again, my patience wearing thin.

She finally sighs and looks up at me, and I'm treated to the sight of her eyes. A light brown color, hazel. Something about them draws me in, like a siren calling to a sailor. Which is equal parts disconcerting and startling.

"I am so very, very sorry," she blurts out. "I didn't mean for that to happen."

"I was expecting an explanation, Ms. Bianchi. Not an apology," I state.

She stares at me for a second and blinks slowly. She's still drunk—not enough to slur her words, thankfully, but drunk enough to confuse strangers for boyfriends she introduces to her parents. Still, the situation is too weird for me to walk away from. And I'm really curious about why she did it.

"I would explain, but I can't even believe what just happened."

"Believe it. Because we're about to walk back into the ballroom, and I guarantee your parents will have questions. Now, do you need me to find your actual boyfriend?" I question.

She shakes her head and mumbles incoherently under her breath. "I don't have one," she finally replies.

I stare at her for several seconds, wondering again what the hell is going on. With a sigh, I rub the bridge of my nose, staring at her.

"Why did you introduce me to your mom as your boyfriend?"

"Because I needed a boyfriend."

"And there wasn't a slew of willing suitors available for the task? Why did you have to wrangle me in?"

She huffs slightly. "I didn't mean to. You just happened to be there."

"Start making sense," I snap.

With an exaggerated sigh, she quickly fills me in on her parents' request that she bring a boyfriend to the party, lest she find herself engaged to Dante Marino. His name inspires only an echo of remembrance. I'm still waiting to hear why I got dragged into it.

"I tried to find someone in time but, surprisingly, it's really hard to find a man to act as my boyfriend—and who my parents would believe I was dating."

"And you thought I was a worthy candidate?" I question, surprised.

"No. I barely even know you. But like I said, you just happened to be there."

I offer her a quizzical look. I'm not sure what to say right now.

"This is a mess," she cries, her head falling into her hands.

I watch her, silently agreeing, while running through the situation in my head. This might be a mess, but somehow— and I really can't believe I got so fucking lucky—the answer to my predicament just landed in my fucking lap. Or, crashed into me. Regardless, Astoria Bianchi, while a bumbling, impulsive oddity of a woman, has provided me with a spectacular opening that I have every intention of exploiting.

"I'll do it," I announce.

She looks up from her wallowing, hazel eyes meeting mine in confusion.

"I'll be your boyfriend," I clarify.

She continues to stare, her expression uncomprehending.

"How much have you had to drink tonight?" I grumble.

"Not much. Not enough for me to understand why a complete stranger is suddenly agreeing to something so crazy."

"But enough for you to introduce said stranger to your mother, without any plans or considerations of what would happen in the aftermath."

She pauses and swears under her breath. "Remind me to never drink tequila again."

"I won't."

She looks at me then, her eyes clearer, studying. "I'm Astoria Bianchi. We might as well introduce ourselves."

"I know who you are," I tell her, holding out my hand.

She places her smaller dainty palm in mine. "Carlo D'Angelo."

She smiles, although it's guarded. "I know who you are, too."

I briefly wonder just how much she actually knows about me.

"Good. Now that the introductions are out of the way, let's head back in," I tell her. She looks alarmed.

"Wait, don't we have to talk? Plan and whatnot?"

My eyes trail over her face. "We've been gone from the party long enough. There's no time to plan."

"But what will we say? My mom has most definitely told my dad what happened. And they'll have questions."

"We're going to walk into the party hand in hand and head over to your parents. Leave the talking to me."

She makes a noise of disagreement. "I'm not comfortable with that."

"Well, I'm not comfortable with being dragged into half-baked schemes by drunk women, and yet…"

Her eyes narrow. "You just expect me to walk in there on your arm and smile like some dumbass while you tell all the lies?"

I nod. "Your words, not mine."

She looks completely against the prospect. She opens her mouth to argue some more but I cut her off by grabbing her wrist.

"You want to sell this to your parents, don't you?" She nods. "Then trust me."

"I don't even know you."

"That's fair. But I'm not doing this out of the goodness of my heart. This arrangement could be mutually beneficial."

"How?" she asks, hazel eyes wide.

"You'll find out later. Just relax."

"I'm the complete opposite of relaxed right now."

"Should I fetch you some more alcohol?"

She glares, but that blessedly keeps her quiet as I maneuver us back into the ballroom. It's still teeming with people, still somehow annoyingly loud. I catch Christian's eye as soon as I enter, and he raises an eyebrow at my new company. I offer him a subtle shake of the head as Astoria and I head over to her parents. They've obviously been waiting for us and are standing to the side, separated from everyone else. Her father casts a disapproving glance at her hand in mine.

"Carlo," he says, authority ringing in his tone. "What the hell is going on?"

A question I've asked myself far too many times this night. Thankfully, Astoria stays quiet as I inform her father that I've been secretly dating his daughter for a few weeks. The emotions on his face flicker from surprise, to confusion, to mild hurt, and then anger.

"How and when did this happen?"

"I'm not sure this is the right place to get into the sordid details, sir. We ran into each other at a restaurant and I was immediately intrigued by her. We ran into each other again and I couldn't help asking her out. Things blossomed from there."

"But I…" He falters. "It doesn't make any sense."

*Trust me, Salvador. I know.*

Her mother, though, seems to have settled in nicely to the idea. She places her hand on her husband's shoulder and smiles. "Come on, my love, you know how these things work. Feelings and emotions are random. They creep on a person."

"Yes, but neither of them has ever given any inclination that they were involved. I wasn't even aware Astoria knew any of the D'Angelos."

My *girlfriend* thankfully chooses this time to step in. "Of course I know them, Daddy. You're always talking about them and when I met Carlo I was curious about the kind of person he is. I didn't tell you because I was worried about how you'd react but then you started talking about me getting engaged to Dante. Carlo and I talked and we agreed it was time to come clean about our relationship."

She places her hand on my chest, making sure to look up at me lovingly. It's a charming display; A-plus for the acting. "Besides, our relationship is still in its early stages. He just asked me out recently."

"They make a wonderful couple, Salvador," her mother says, beaming.

Thank God she's somehow accepting this farce of a relationship. Otherwise we'd have encountered much stronger opposition. Salvador doesn't look nearly as amenable.

"Sure," he says gruffly. His brown eyes are narrowed in suspicion. "Does your bid to purchase my building have anything to do with this sudden... development?"

*Absolutely.*

"No. I deliberately didn't mention my relationship because I didn't want it to interfere with the negotiations. The building has nothing to do with how I feel," I say, mustering complete sincerity in my tone.

He still doesn't look convinced. He turns to his daughter. "A D'Angelo, Astoria. Really?"

"He's standing right here, Dad," she says with a smile. "You love them."

"I loved their father. The lot of them, though, I'm not so sure anymore," Salvador corrects, eyeing me.

I offer my best attempt at a charming smile. He sighs.

"We need to talk more about this," he states.

33

"Not today," Camelia interjects. "Carlo, you should join us for dinner. When are you free?"

I mentally run through my schedule. "I have matters to attend to for most of this week," I say apologetically. "Would next Tuesday be alright?"

Astoria lightly jabs her elbow into my side. "Babe," she says with a nervous laugh, "I have a night shift at the hospital on Tuesdays, remember?"

Of course I don't fucking remember, seeing as I had no idea she worked at a hospital. I vaguely remember someone mentioning she's a doctor but it slipped my mind.

I quickly gloss over the slip-up. "Right. How about Wednesday, then?"

Both her parents nod and Astoria doesn't offer any objections. After one last glance at the both of us, Salvador and Camelia walk away to continue playing darling hosts. Christian catches my eye from across the room and points at his watch—a clear sign that we have to go. I notice he has managed to wrangle Topher to his side and my sister-in-laws as well. They're all watching curiously.

I inwardly sigh. This situation will be a bitch to explain.

I turn to Astoria. "You're meeting me tomorrow," I inform her.

She doesn't even argue. "I'm free for lunch. Does two work?"

I nod. "I'll text you the details."

She arches a dark eyebrow. "You don't even have my number."

"You'll find, Ms. Bianchi, that there's not a lot of things that are out of my reach. Getting your number will be a piece of cake."

"I probably should have found myself a boyfriend with a bit less ego," she muses.

"Tomorrow," I say, ignoring her statement. She rolls her eyes and waves me away.

Instead of leaving, I pull her closer and place a soft kiss on her forehead, right under the dark tendrils of her hair. I don't miss the way she stiffens or the slight hitch in her breath.

"Your parents are watching," I explain when she looks up at me in question. We've also garnered the attention of half the guests in the room, but I ignore them. "Good night, Ms. Bianchi."

I walk away without another glance, wondering again just how I got myself into this situation.

# CHAPTER 5

*Tori*

From what I've heard, the best dreams are the ones you forget fastest. They fade almost immediately, the feelings they elicit falling away. For me, it's the opposite. My nightmares evoke the same reaction. I guess I should be glad. When I wake up, I get to forget it all. When I wake up, all the fear and terror is gone. It's like shedding a layer of my skin. When I wake up, I get to be normal. When I wake up, I'm not broken.

---

THE GRAVITY of my actions hits me the next morning as I fade between consciousness and subconsciousness. Then I remember everything and I'm blasted out of sleep. I sit up in my bed and groan.

*Fuck.*

"I'm going to make myself feel better by assigning a large portion of blame for last night's activities to tequila," I mutter aloud, staring at the digital clock at my side.

I woke up five minutes earlier than usual. My subconscious brain had been dreaming up scenarios where Carlo D'Angelo shot me for my behavior last night.

After he and his family left, I managed to find an older woman willing to fill me in on every bit of news, gossip, everything that's known about the D'Angelo family. By the time she was done, I was feeling a little squeamish—although I'm not sure if that had to do with the tequila or the story of the D'Angelos' ruthless murders.

They're a scary bunch, and apparently, Carlo's the worst of them all. Not just because of his ruthlessness but because of how little is known about him. He's mysterious, intimidating, and probably the worst candidate I could have picked for a fake boyfriend. I'm still not sure why he agreed to the ruse.

I spent the rest of the night dodging my parents' questions. After the party, we headed home and I retired to my room, falling asleep immediately.

With a sigh, I head to the shower and get ready for the day. Luckily for me, my parents like to sleep in, so I'm able to have a quick breakfast and leave the house before they can barrage me with more questions. Questions I don't have an answer to.

The hospital's busy, and I'm soon too overcome with work to think about my new predicament. Until I get a text from an unknown number.

> Reese's café, Oakland Avenue. 2 p.m., Ms. Bianchi. Don't be late.

There's no need to ask who it is but I do so anyway. My text is quickly followed by a bland reply.

> Carlo D'Angelo. Save my number.

It doesn't escape my notice that the café he chose is close

enough to the hospital that I can walk there. I'm glad. I was worried I'd have to battle New York traffic to get to wherever he chose.

> Me: How did you get my number?

Carlo: For someone who didn't ask any questions before dragging me into a terribly concocted lie, you sure have a lot of questions for me.

Mr. D'Angelo's certainly a snarky sort, and I have a feeling he's one to hold grudges.

> Me: You don't seem to mind being dragged into my lie right now. I want to know why.

Carlo: 2 p.m., Ms. Bianchi.

I huff out a breath at the elusive reply, then console myself with the knowledge that I'll at least have answers to my questions when we meet up.

Carlo's unsurprisingly punctual and I'm met with him already seated and looking impatient when I arrive at the café, ten minutes late.

"I'm a doctor," I say when he continues to stare at me judgmentally. "Emergencies come up a lot in my line of work. I didn't mean to arrive late."

"Duly noted," he says dryly. "Have a seat."

My eyes travel to the peaked lapels of his black suit, sans tie, to the open collar of his crisp white shirt and the tanned skin peeking through. I quickly look away.

"Why are you dressed so formally?" I question, unable to stop myself.

I'm wearing scrubs but I realize I should've opted for a

casual look and a white coat I could've simply removed before meeting with Carlo. He looks like he's about to present a slideshow in front of a board of executives while looking dashingly handsome.

I hate that I noticed how handsome he is.

His eyes flicker to my face. "I work for the mafia, Ms. Bianchi. This is adequate attire for my job."

I tense at the cavalier way with which he just admitted to his life of crime and start to question whether it's a good idea to continue down this possibly destructive path. Then I notice Carlo's eyes are still on me, watching intently. He's waiting for a reaction.

I clear my throat, feigning calm and refusing to give him the satisfaction of one.

"Right," I say. "Let's just get this over with."

"This isn't something to be gotten over with, considering the delicacy of the situation. If we're doing this, we need to do it right. Are we clear, Ms. Bianchi? No more throwing yourself at random strangers."

I feel like a schoolgirl being scolded. Heat blossoms in my cheeks. "I did not throw myself at you. And stop calling me that!"

"What?"

"Ms. Bianchi. My name is Astoria. Everyone calls me Tori, though."

"Tori, then. I'll have to get familiar with it, considering you're going to be my girlfriend. You can call me Carlo."

"Oh, I'm so pleased to have your permission to call you by your legal first name which everyone calls you by. Such a privilege," I say sarcastically.

He's the picture of relaxed elegance as he leans back into his seat, his brown eyes sharp. "Explain to me again why you need a fake boyfriend."

I'm not sure I want to spill all the dirty details of my situation to him, but something about the look in his eyes loosens my tongue and I find myself spilling the entire story.

"What's so unappealing about Marino?" Carlo questions.

I shrug, "I couldn't say. I don't really know the man. But I've had a few run-ins with him and my instincts are telling me he's someone I should stay away from. I always listen to my instincts."

Carlo throws me a weighted glance. "And what are those instincts saying about me?"

"They're not tingling as much as they do around Dante," I admit.

Now, he looks amused.

"Interesting." He doesn't press the subject, instead moving along to other problems involving our situation. "We need a good story. How did we meet? Where? We need to figure out the little details that your parents or anyone else might ask about."

I tuck a loose curl that's fallen out back into my messy bun as I consider that. "I'm usually busy with work during the weekdays, so a Saturday? I had dinner with a friend at La Vie a month ago. We could claim to have met then."

He nods in agreement. "Alright. We met at La Vie. Then what happened?"

"Um… you were so dazzled by my beautiful face that you asked me out on a date?"

His expression is bland as he stares at me. "Doubtful. You don't know me, Ms. Bianchi, but trust me, that wouldn't be the case."

"What are you suggesting, then?"

He leans closer, his eyes still neutral, thoughtful. "You approached me because you've always wanted to meet me. After all the years of hearing about me and my family, you were curious. We had a conversation, there were sparks, but we didn't see each other again until a few days later."

I make a face but when his eyes meet mine, daring me to provide an alternate option, my mouth clamps shut. "Alright. So we met up a few days later and started dating?"

Carlo shakes his head. "No, if this thing is going to work, we can't have been dating for more than two weeks. I thought it over last night."

"What? Why?"

His eyes trail over my face, and he takes his sweet time answering the question. "Because I was involved with someone else around that time."

"Oh," I mutter. I don't know why I'm so surprised. Of course, he's allowed to have been in a relationship. I just never considered it. Plus, he seems so closed-off, I guess I can't imagine him dating anybody. "Alright. I'm just a little worried. My parents are supposed to believe this thing between us is real and serious, even though we've only known each other for a few weeks."

"They'll believe it."

"Really? Because for some reason, my dad's already really suspicious. Which brings us to my next question," I state. "Why are you doing this?"

He shrugs. "There's no reason. I'm doing this out of the kindness of my heart, Ms. Bianchi."

"Ha-ha, very funny."

His blank expression doesn't flicker as he finally answers. "I need something from your father. My brother and I have been trying to procure a building from him. But he's saying he'll only give it to his son-in-law as a wedding gift."

"The building in Bayside?" I say warily, remembering earlier conversations with my dad over it. Carlo nods.

It's a pretty big building, in a really good neighborhood.

My dad has mentioned his plans with the building to me before but I've never really thought about it. I guess it makes sense that they'd want it, but my dad can be pretty stubborn. Once he decides on something, it's almost impossible to change his mind.

"Alright, your reason checks out. One tiny chink in your plan, though—there's no way I'm walking down the aisle and actually making you his son-in-law."

A smile flickers over his mouth. "Don't worry, Ms. Bianchi. All you have to do is act like my loving girlfriend. I'll take care of the rest."

I'm not sure what exactly he plans to do. But I have a feeling with him, the less I know, the better.

"Fine. I guess we're doing this. Also, it's Tori. T-O-R-I, Tori," I remind him, slightly exasperated.

He rolls his eyes. "We need a formal agreement."

"Like a written contract with regard to our fake relationship?" I ask. He nods once and I huff. "Is that really necessary?"

Carlo arches an eyebrow. "I never make a deal without carefully laying everything out."

"We can do that. But a written contract is overkill. We're starting a fake relationship, you're not recruiting me into the mafia."

His cool gaze flicks over my face. "Definitely not."

"Let's just lay out the rules. First, one has to cover physical contact," I start, feeling my cheeks heat. "We'll have to touch a lot and maybe a kiss or two."

"A kiss or two," Carlo repeats blandly, although his brown eyes flicker in amusement.

"Yes. There will absolutely be no sex," I say firmly.

"Don't worry, Ms. Bianchi. I have no interest in sleeping with you."

I ignore the slight twinge of disappointment at his words. He didn't have to be so blunt about it.

"Okay. Do you have any conditions of your own?"

"No pictures. Or posting me on social media."

"That's not an issue." I ponder my next words, hesitating slightly. "No violence," I say carefully. When he arches an eyebrow, I explain, "I'm a doctor, Carlo. I am not and will never be comfortable watching you beat someone up."

"Yes, because I tend to do that a lot," he drawls.

"Do you not?" I counter, to which he shrugs.

"No violence when you're around, except special circumstances that may warrant them," he states, offering me a compromise.

I suppose it's as good as I'm going to get. We talk a little more about the more delicate chinks in our plan.

"We need to be more comfortable with each other. You can't be so... rigid all the time," I inform him.

"I have no idea what you're talking about," he says, even as tension rolls through his shoulders.

I get the feeling Carlo D'Angelo never relaxes, ever. He always has to be in control, and on top of everything.

"This isn't going to work if you can't act like you love me," I state.

He looks appalled by the idea, and I sigh softly. This might not go as smoothly as we hope.

"Have you ever been in love?" I ask.

Carlo rolls his eyes before getting to his feet. "We're done for today," he says, ignoring my question.

It's pretty clear he's put up a wall; I can see the change in his body language. I stand as well.

"We'll meet again tomorrow," Carlo says, and I arch an eyebrow. "So we can practice getting comfortable with each other before we see your parents," he clarifies.

"Right. A week should be plenty of time to get used to each other."

He nods. "I can't see you again after tomorrow, though. I'll be swamped with work."

"No problem. But I get to pick the time and location for tomorrow," I tell him, smiling.

"Let me know by tonight."

And with that, he leaves, not even so much as a word of goodbye. He could work on his manners. Scratch that, he could work on his entire sense of self. Despite all that, I'm actually curious.

Carlo doesn't strike me as a man who often lets people see beyond the surface. But if this is going to work, he's going to have to give at least a little in that regard.

It just might be interesting to watch him crack.

# CHAPTER 6

*Carlo*

The club is silent as I walk through the halls, heading for the double doors that lead into the quiet room. There's a woman in front of it, wearing shorts and a shirt that leaves nothing to the imagination. Her blue eyes are blank as she gives me a nod and a smile. She hands me a glass of whiskey, already used to my order, and then she leaves.

I've been coming to this place for more than five years. Secrecy is key among the members. It's an underground club where men can come and fulfill their debased desires without judgment. Men with something to hide. I'm not sure who half the other members are, and frankly, I don't care. I started coming here to get some peace and quiet. Plus, it afforded me time to hang out with one of the few people in the world, apart from my family, that I have any sort of regard for.

Cool green eyes that had been locked onto a phone lift to stare at me. Khalil offers me a small smile as I take the seat opposite him. There's a tumbler filled with ice, a champagne bottle, and a glass on the table between us. He got started without me.

"You're late," he says or rather accuses because punctuality is of the utmost importance to him.

"I got held up."

He gives me a wry stare. "By the Bianchi girl, I'm guessing."

I'm not surprised he knows. Khalil Larsen is a legend in our world. Not because of who he is but what he is. And what he is, is practically a ghost. He's a genius when it comes to keeping himself invisible. He owns a private investigations company, but what he does is mostly off the books. He's able to keep up his lifestyle because he's quite frankly the best hacker I've ever met.

Christian would be amazed by what Khalil can do. They have never met before. Khalil values anonymity, and he never steps out of the shadows unless he wants to. Which is why this friendship works so well.

"What did you find out?"

"There are whispers everywhere, of course. A D'Angelo with a Bianchi. You just might make the front pages of the top gossip magazines."

My lips curl in distaste. "I'd rather not."

"I figured. I made a few calls, wiped a few servers, and stopped all the articles. The relevant ones anyway. Now you owe me a favor."

"Of course," I say, gesturing with my glass for him to continue.

"Explain this farce of a relationship to me," he prompts.

I roll my eyes, unsurprised. I offer him the quick details and by the time I'm done, he's amused.

"So you're tying yourself to her to procure a building."

"It's mutually beneficial," I say on a shrug.

"From what I know, fake relationships never end well."

"And why's that?"

"Because somehow the parties involved always fall for each other."

I flinch slightly before looking him in the eye. "I'm confident that's not going to happen."

Khalil's still amused. Dark eyes trail over my face. "I was going to go to London for a while, but maybe I'll stick around. See how this goes."

I arch an eyebrow at that. "You're going to stick around because you expect me to somehow fall for a woman I barely know and have no interest in pursuing a relationship with."

"I'm sticking around because you're playing with fire and it'll be funny if mister made of steel gets burnt."

"Why the hell do I keep you around, Larsen?" I question, bringing my glass to my lips.

He smiles. "Because you'd be practically useless without me. Even now, you want me to do something for you."

I shrug. He knows me well. "I need info on Salvador Bianchi."

"What kind of info?"

"The damning kind."

This time, when Khalil smiles, it's mischievous. "You're planning on blackmailing your future father-in-law?"

"Shut up. It's only a backup plan. Just in case. And he's not my future father-in-law," I add.

"Mmm," Khalil says.

"So you'll do it?"

"Fine. I'm only doing this because you took care of the McLaren case for me."

I nod. "Consider us even."

We're never even for long. Eventually, one of us owes the other. We've founded a relationship based on mutual usefulness and something else: trust. Because I could tell Khalil my deepest, darkest secrets and the bastard wouldn't blink. I don't tell him everything, but there's a great comfort in having a confidant.

"So, tell me more about the Bianchi girl. You think she's hot, don't you?"

My eyebrows rise. "Fuck off, Larsen."

"No, seriously. I'm curious about exactly what you think of her."

My mind goes back to our conversation in the café. Astoria Bianchi's definitely not like most other women. With her, you never know what to expect. Which, more than anything, is what turns me off about her. I value clear lines and precision. She's a disaster waiting to happen.

And yet, I need her in order to get what I want.

"She's a means to an end," I tell Khalil.

"But you think she's beautiful. I've seen some pictures and oof." He whistles.

"Of course, I think she's beautiful. I have eyes," I say, only to get him off my back. Khalil's a dog with a bone when he wants something. Relentless.

He looks pleased at my admission. "Yes, you have eyes. But I'm wondering if you've still got a heart buried under all this."

I have a heart—it's a shabby, worn thing, probably, but it's there. I ignore Khalil's statement and we continue to have a drink, peaceful quiet between us. An hour later, I'm heading home, and my phone pings with a text as I head into my apartment. It's from Astoria.

> Astoria: 6 p.m., Earling Bar. Don't be late. I can only be there for an hour before I have to head back to the hospital.

I quickly type out a reply and send.

48

> Me: I'm not going to a bar, Ms. Bianchi.

> Astoria: TORI!!

She texts back in all caps to punctuate her frustration. I smirk. It's kind of entertaining to rile her up.

> Astoria: What does your royal highness have against bars, anyway?

I can practically hear the dryness of her tone. My reply is brief.

> Me: I'm not a fan of being out in public.

> Astoria: Of course you're not. Suck it up, Carlo. It's just a bar.

> Me: Why is your first choice a place loaded with alcohol? I'm starting to think you have a problem.

> Astoria: I really don't like what you're implying, Mr. D'Angelo. It's not like I was planning on drinking!

Despite myself, I smile.

> Me: Counterproposal?

> Astoria: Fine, let's hear it.

> Me: How about I pick you up after work? You said you have the night shift. I can drop you off at your parents' home.

She doesn't reply for several seconds. I drop my phone on

the dresser and begin to undress. Once her reply comes, I pick it up.

> Astoria: I'll be done pretty late. Around 2 in the morning. Are you sure you want to forgo your sleep for this?

> Me: I can manage, Ms. Bianchi.

> Astoria: Alright. You can pick me up at the hospital. I would tell you where it is, but I'm sure you already know.

> Me: Smart woman.

> Astoria: See you tomorrow, Carlo.

I hesitate before texting back.

> Me: Good night.

So far so good. This arrangement might not be the headache I was so worried it would be. As long as Astoria and I continue to act civil with one another, things might actually turn out alright.

---

THE NEXT DAY comes with a list of problems. A few of our men are arrested in the middle of striking a lucrative deal. The forestalling of the deal costs us a lot of money and the station they're being held at is refusing to release them. Something about orders from the higher-ups. Someone in the FBI is keeping an eye on the case.

With gritted teeth, I text my youngest brother.

> Me: Tell your father-in-law to lay off us.

His reply is instantaneous.

> Topher: I'll see what I can do but you know
> how he is. Whatever's wrong, I'm sure you
> and the Don will sort it out.

I sigh. This isn't an issue we can solve tonight. James Malone's an unrelenting hard man. One would think that his daughter joining our family would cause him to be a little more lenient, but it's been the opposite. He's working even harder to hit us from every angle. It's really starting to piss me off. The men in custody might just have to settle for some time in jail. I'll make sure they're compensated adequately.

I inform Christian of the development, and he tells me he'll look into it. By the time I'm able to leave the precinct, it's time to pick up Astoria. I briefly wonder if it's a good idea to even see her. I'm on edge, considering everything that's happened today, and a little angry. Still, it's too late to cancel our plans now.

As soon as I arrive at the parking lot, I send a text informing her that I'm here. But she doesn't reply. I wait for ten minutes before my patience runs out. I head for the front desk. The woman behind it raises an eyebrow as I approach.

"Can I help you?" she questions.

"I was wondering where Dr. Bianchi is?"

Calling her a doctor feels weird. It hits me that I've really separated a part of her life from my overall sense of who she is.

The woman's eyes grow wide. "I'm sorry and you are?"

"Her boyfriend," I reply, glad that the lie flows easily past my lips.

Her eyes widen further. "I'm sorry, what?"

I don't repeat myself.

"Are you going to tell me where she is or not?" I question tiredly.

She nods, though her eyes are narrowed suspiciously. "Fourth floor. She should be wrapping up her rounds by now. Her office is the third door on the right."

I head for the elevator. There's no one walking the hallways of the third floor when I arrive, and I immediately head for the door the receptionist directed me to. The plaque in front reads, 'resident's office.' When I knock, though, there's no reply. It's not like I can just barge in. I call her, but she doesn't pick up her phone.

With a frustrated huff, I walk out into the hallway and eventually find myself in front of the children's ward. A voice has my footsteps halting. Her voice. So I stay out of sight beside the entrance to the ward and listen.

"So I have to use drugs every day forever?" comes a tiny feminine voice.

Astoria laughs softly. There's some rustling and then she's speaking to the little girl, her voice gentle.

"Of course not. Just until you get better, sweetheart."

"And how long will that take?" the little girl counters.

Astoria doesn't reply for a long moment. "As long as it takes, Sarah. As long as it takes until you feel better and your tummy doesn't hurt anymore."

Sarah sighs softly. "I hate being sick."

"Yeah, it's not a picnic." Astoria laughs.

"Thank you, Doctor Tori."

"For what?"

"For taking care of me," the little girl replies.

"I'm your doctor honey. That's my job. Yours is to relax and focus on getting better ok?"

There's some quiet for a minute or two before I hear some more rustling.

"I have to go home now. It's pretty late and you should be sleeping. Right now, there's probably a very angry man waiting for me downstairs."

Sarah laughs. "Why is he angry?"

"Because I'm late. He hates it when I'm late but between me and you, he hates everything," she chuckles.

"But you're doing your job. He should understand."

Astoria sighs. "He should, but I doubt he will."

*Great. Way to make me feel good about myself.*

"You on the other hand, are a bright young lady who is asking way too many questions when you should be resting. Goodnight, I will be here to check on you tomorrow," she says.

It takes me a moment to realize Astoria's already walking out. When her eyes land on me, they widen. I quickly close my hand over her opened mouth before she can scream. I doubt Sarah's the only kid in there. I pull her toward the wall and step in front of her. After a few seconds, I raise an eyebrow in question, and she nods to tell me she's composed herself.

I release the hand covering her mouth and she immediately hits my chest. My eyes narrow.

"What the hell are you doing here?" she whisper-shouts.

"You wouldn't pick up your phone."

"So you decided to go stalking about a hospital?"

"I was looking for you."

"And you were eavesdropping. What did you hear?"

"Nothing. Let's go," I tell her. "You can explain why you decided to leave your phone wherever the hell you left it."

She follows me as I start walking down the hallway toward her office. When we arrive, I cross my arms and wait for her to open it. She does. I don't follow her inside but when she exits, she has taken off her white coat and a purse slung over her shoulder. She peers at me.

"I still want to know what you heard."

"Let's go, Doctor Bianchi."

"Oh, so it's *Doctor* Bianchi now, is it?"

"Yes," I say without looking at her as I head for the elevators.

For some reason, after listening to her conversation with that little girl, I'm not sure how to act around her anymore.

# CHAPTER 7

*Tori*

The car ride home is quiet and it's stifling and I hate it. Carlo seems like the kind of man who thrives in silence, but I'm starting to feel suffocated. When I decide I can't take it anymore, I reach for the car stereo and he slaps my hand away.

"Ow!" I yell in indignation.

"No," he says in that dry way of his. "The only person who gets to play music in my car is me."

I glare at the side of his face. "You're an asshole."

He hums in reply. I'm starting to think this car ride was a bad idea. He's irritable and I'm exhausted.

A few minutes later, Carlo asks, "What's wrong with the kid back there?"

My eyes flicker to his face but his expression is blank.

"Sarah?"

He nods.

"She has Cancer. Stomach Cancer."

"There's no cure?" Carlo questions.

I shake my head as something painful grips my heart.

"No. It's localized but she's having a hard time with the treatment so we're trying a few different approaches.

It's just so frustrating. I hate that she has to go through all that."

"I'm sure you're doing the best you can."

"You're being weirdly nice," I say, shooting him a look.

He rolls his eyes. "You're impossible to please. Exactly what do you want from me?"

I shrug. "I just want to get to know you."

That gives him pause. "Why?"

"Because it'll help with our deal. Plus, I have a feeling we could be friends."

Now he's visibly surprised. "Friends? We're complete opposites. What I just witnessed at the hospital is clear evidence of that."

"How can you be so sure? That we're opposites," I question.

"Trust me, our moral compasses point in completely different directions."

He might be right about that. But I'm sure we could find common ground.

"Still, we could try."

He might seem a little rough around the edges, but that's honestly making me all the more curious about him.

"From fake girlfriend to friend, huh?" he asks, his gaze still fixed on the road.

"Our relationship is progressing wonderfully."

Somehow, that manages to draw a smile out of him. And making him smile feels like a personal victory. We arrive at my parents' house and I step out of the car, looking at him through the window.

"What time should I arrive for dinner next week?" he questions.

"Seven. And wear a tie. It'll make you look responsible."

"I always look responsible," he argues.

"No, you always look like a sulky mafia boss. Which you are."

"Christian's the don," he reminds me.

"Yeah, but it's clear that you're the real boss."

Besides, we're trying to win points with my dad. Wear a tie."

He sighs like it's the worst suggestion in the world. "Fine."

"See. Life would be so much easier if you were more amenable to my suggestions."

"Don't hold your breath, Astoria."

I smile. I like the sound of my name on his lips.

Before he drives away, my eyes meet his brown ones. "I'm sorry I left my phone behind. I should have known you'd be calling but I lost track of time. I'll try to be much more efficient when it comes to communication from now on as long as it does not interfere with my job. If anything, I'll send a quick text next time."

Carlo's eyes brighten in surprise. He starts the car, but not before tossing one last look at me.

"Life would be so much easier if you were always this agreeable and apologetic."

"Don't hold your breath, Carlo."

He gives me a short nod before driving away. I watch his car exit the estate before heading inside the house. Thankfully, my parents are still awake when I walk in. They're in the living room, watching a show. I get to brag that my very amazing boyfriend picked me up from work and dropped me off. My mother beams, but my dad casts me a very suspicious look.

I'm hoping that once they get to meet him officially, his

doubts will be quieted and we'll be able to finally convince him that this is real.

---

I WASN'T KIDDING when I told Carlo I'd try to communicate well. The few days we don't see each other are spent texting back and forth. At first, I was just trying to find out random information about him—his birthday, or things that could come up about his family. Then we started talking about common areas of interest. He likes to play pool. He gambles on occasion, which wasn't surprising. He's actually not that bad once you get to know him. He's funny in a droll sort of way, and intelligent, and... I force myself to stop thinking about Carlo and instead try to look forward to tonight.

He'll be here in a few minutes.

A family dinner like this happens once every two weeks. We never really have much time to hang out. My dad's busy managing a his companies, my mother's busy working as a vice-president at Union Bank, and I'm busy at the hospital. But we've made it a rule to sit for dinner at least twice a month and have a conversation as a family. Usually, I love our family dinners.

However, I have a feeling today's dinner isn't going to go as smoothly as they usually do.

As always, Carlo's annoyingly punctual. By 7 p.m., he's driving onto the grounds, so I step outside to meet him. There's an unwanted feeling in my gut as I take him in. He's in a navy-blue suit that's perfectly tailored with crisp lines, although I feel a little disappointment when I notice he's not wearing a tie.

"Hey," I say, walking up to him.

He offers me a small smile before holding out a finger. He

quickly pokes his head into the car to grab something, and when he retreats, he's holding a tie in his hands. Just like that, my mood brightens.

"I wasn't sure how to knot it. I could have learned but I figured since you're the architect of this situation, you might as well take care of it."

"I can't believe you're admitting you can't do something."

"I never said I couldn't. I just don't want to."

"Yeah, yeah."

I fail to hide my smile as I grab the tie from his hand, stepping closer until I'm standing in front of him. We've never been this close before. My heart skips a beat as I take in his face. There's a small scar on his jaw that I hadn't noticed. And his nose is a little crooked, like it's been broken before. Those small imperfections only serve to make him more appealing, though.

When Carlo raises an eyebrow, I realize I've been staring, and I quickly get to work on knotting the tie. He leans down slightly so I can do so, considering he's much taller than me.

"You look beautiful, by the way," he says gruffly.

I picked out a black dress and wore it without much thought because I was nervous about tonight. But his comment warns my heart regardless.

"Thank you," I murmur, hating how my cheeks heat at his words.

Once I'm done with the tie, I step back to admire my handiwork.

"There, now you look like the man of my dreams," I say sarcastically.

He looks like a creature of the night stepping into the light. But I keep that to myself. It'll only reinforce his belief that we're opposites, and I'm of the firm belief that nothing's ever black or white. There are gray areas, and Carlo has his as well.

"Come on, *dolcezza*. Let's go meet the parents," he says.

With surprising ease, he wraps his hand around my waist. The touch burns, but I don't flinch. I really have grown comfortable with him. While most people would be unable to relax in his presence, I find I can do that fairly easily. It's odd.

My parents are in the kitchen when we walk in. Family night signifies the one night where my mom actually uses the kitchen. The staff usually excuse us while we take care of dinner on our own.

We walk in on them speaking.

"Be nice, Salvador," my mom is saying, but she falls silent when they notice us at the doorway.

"Mom, Dad," I say, looking at each of them.

Their eyes are fixed on Carlo, and I don't miss the unfriendly look my father gives him. Damn, he's really not taking this well.

"Mr. and Mrs. Bianchi," Carlo greets politely. "You have a wonderful home."

"You used to spend a lot of time here when you were little," Mom says, walking forward and pulling him into a hug. "Though I doubt you'd remember. I was pregnant with Tori then. You were only four. Christian was a baby, so he was usually with your mother, but you always used to follow your dad around. Remember, Salvador?" she asks, jabbing her elbow into my dad's stomach.

He glares at her briefly before turning to us. "Right. From what I remember, you and Carman were practically inseparable as you grew up."

When I look at Carlo, I notice the way he's tensed. It's not particularly obvious. His face is still a blank, polite mask but

I can tell he's uncomfortable with the topic of discussion. I quickly change it.

"So, what are we having for dinner?"

I walk in further and my mom and I start discussing what we could cook. We quickly put the men to work cutting vegetables and setting the table. Cooking together is our way of bonding. Carlo gives no indication of being uncomfortable with it. He does everything my mother asks without complaint. Dinner's ready in an hour and we all move to the dining table to eat.

"So, Carlo," my dad begins, "how's work in the Cosa Nostra?"

I shoot him a subtle glare. Seriously? In what world is that polite dinner conversation?

For his part, Carlo simply shrugs, looking him in the eye as he replies. "Mostly managerial duties, sir. Christian's in charge of running the family, I just assist him to the best of my ability."

"I've heard of your contributions over the years. Christian might be in charge, but you've really taken a firm hand in dealing with things."

"I do my best," he says simply.

He doesn't seem bothered by people bringing up what he does or what his family business involves. Most people would shy away from speaking of such a profession, but Carlo seems almost proud.

"Dad, aren't you going to ask me about my work?" I question, changing the topic of conversation again.

My dad turns to me, his brown eyes growing warm. "Of course, honey. How are things at the hospital?"

My mother butts in before I can reply. "Sometimes I still can't believe she went to medical school and stuck with it," she says to Carlo with a smile. "She used to tell us all the time that one day, she'd be a doctor, but her father and I thought it was just a phase. She stuck with it, though. When she wants something, Astoria can be quite relentless."

"You should be proud of her," Carlo says. "She's a wonderful doctor, kind and selfless. She really cares about her patients."

The words are an exaggeration since Carlo's only known me for a few days, but it still nice to hear. I shoot him a small smile and he smiles back tenderly. The sight of it has my heart flipping, so I reach for some water to distract myself from him. My parents are staring at us, their gazes curious. Well, mostly my dad. As for my mom, she has really settled into the idea of this relationship.

"We are more than proud of Astoria's accomplishments," she says. "I must admit, her father and I used to be so worried. For the longest time, she only cared about her work. Imagine our surprise when she told us she was seeing someone. But the two of you look wonderful together. I'm glad you found each other."

And there it is. I feel something like a fist tightening around my chest. Guilt. In the long run, this is a good idea— if I wasn't doing this with Carlo, my parents would have kept pushing for me to get engaged to Dante Marino. But that doesn't mean I like lying to them. Mom seems genuinely happy and I hate that it's all fake.

The conversation shifts to other things—the story of how we met, how Carlo asked me out. He's quite adept at lying, embellishing the stories at the right moments and even sneaking in some jokes to make my mother laugh. Eventually, even my dad starts to relax. When we're done with dinner, we both offer to do the dishes but my mom insists we leave it for the staff so we can enjoy our night together. We had already gladly made our way into the kitchen when my other called us over.

It doesn't take long before we're joining my parents in the living room. Carlo moves out of the way for me to sit down, then takes a seat right next to me. I wrap my arms around his neck and smile, the picture of a happy couple.

"Where do you live, Carlo?" my mom questions.

He tells her and she beams, her expression suddenly growing mischievous.

"I have an idea," she announces. "Tori, darling, you're always talking about how hard it is to get to the hospital every day since the house is so far away. Why don't you just move in with Carlo? You've been talking about moving out for a while now," she says but I can't tell if this is one of her attempts at making a joke or not.

My mouth drops open. Carlo freezes. "Mom," I say in surprise.

"What?" she asks innocently. "I'm just joking."

"We've only been officially dating for around two weeks. We're trying to take things slowly, Mother."

Dad pipes up, "She's right. Relationships shouldn't be rushed, *mi amor*."

That's rich coming from a person who wanted me engaged to a man I barely know. I catch the teasing glint in Carlo's eyes that tells me he's thinking the exact same thing. I lean closer and whisper in his ear.

"Do you want to get out of here? We could go check out my bedroom," I suggest, feeling like a teenager with her first boyfriend.

I just need to get us out of here before my parents bring up marriage.

"Sure," he says easily.

I stand up, momentarily disappointed by the loss of heat

from sitting so close to him. We inform my parents I'm going to give Carlo a tour so he can see the upgrades we've made since he was a kid. I lead Carlo up the stairs, opening the door to my bedroom. A relieved breath leaves me and then I'm falling onto my bed with a sigh.

"You did well," he mutters, closing the door and leaning against it.

I sit up. "You think so? I think Dad's come to accept it."

"Yeah, there were a lot less glares from him toward the end."

I laugh before quickly sobering. "Sorry for dragging you into all this. I know it's a lot."

"Mutually beneficial, remember?"

I pat the side of my bed, gesturing for him to come sit. He arches an amused eyebrow, shuffling closer and sitting down.

"Nice room," Carlo says, taking in the surroundings.

"Don't judge. This has been my room for most of my existence," I tell him.

"It's cute." He smiles when he notices the Hannah Montana poster in the corner.

I groan softly. "My mom was right when she said I was considering moving out of the house. I've been considering it since I started my residency. Only problem is, I'm not the biggest fan of change. Every time I look at apartments, I manage to convince myself that they're not what I want or they're not good enough."

"I could help you look if you wanted," Carlo offers. "Or we could ask my mother for help. The woman's a shark. Put her in charge of it and she'll bulldoze through the entire process, even going so far as to picking out all the furniture. She's the one that helped me with my apartment."

"You never talk about your family," I say with a smile.

He shrugs. "I'm a private guy."

"Understatement. But how is your mom? Does she know about all this?"

"No, I didn't tell her anything. She's currently out of the country. These days, she spends most of her time in Milan. She left a month ago. Her sister lives there. *Mamma* gets a little lonely when she's here."

There's warmth in his voice when he talks about his mother.

"But the rest of your family knows?"

"I didn't tell them much. That night after the party, they all badgered me for details until I told them we were entering into an arrangement. I eventually explained what was going on to Christian. I'm sure he filled them in."

"Oh, good, so they know it's a fake relationship. I was worried we'd need to keep up appearances around them as well."

"That's not necessary," he informs me

We fall silent and I lie down, looking up at the ceiling. I'm curious about something and while a part of me knows I shouldn't ask, the question leaves my lips regardless.

"What was your relationship with your dad like?"

Carlo tenses. He doesn't look at me, and I internally berate myself. Tonight was going so well.

# CHAPTER 8

*Carlo*

Carman D'Angelo was a great man. He lived his life so that he would be great in every manner. My father never did anything or embarked on anything that wouldn't succeed. He left his mark on everyone, in many different ways.

Christian became like him, forever chasing after his legacy and trying his best to be like him. On the flip side, Topher did and still does everything to stay away from exactly that. I guess I'm somewhere in the middle. The only difference is my father groomed me differently. He taught and showed me things that my brothers couldn't fathom. He wanted me to live life without fear but to be feared and ruthless so that I could always protect the others. As the first son of the don, you learn quickly that life is full of evil and darkness. The shitty part about it is a lot of it, comes from us. Even as a kid, I was my fathers right hand man and when you spend your entire life being your father's bitch, his death sets you free.

I loved my old man, but losing him freed me of the expectations that have always felt like a noose around my neck.

Everyone thought I would be upset that he chose Christian to be his successor, maybe even angry. All I felt was relief. Christian was always better suited for the position. And I've always been better suited to the shadows. I'd do anything for my little brother—anything but take the burden off his shoulders. I guess that was dad's plan all along.

I don't tell Astoria any of this, however. I understand her parents' inquisitiveness, but she should know there's a line that shouldn't be crossed.

"That's none of your business, *dolcezza*," I state.

Her eyes narrow. "It was a harmless question. No need to get your panties in a twist."

Her tone annoys me and I get to my feet.

"Come on, let's go see your parents. I need to leave."

She's visibly upset as I lead us back downstairs. While a part of me feels bad for ruining the cool, easy way things had been going, another part of me is glad. Lines were getting blurred way too fast and I was getting too comfortable in her presence. I need to keep my eyes on the goal.

The Bianchi family escorts me outside. Her parents stay at the doorway while Astoria accompanies me to my car. When I look back at her parents, whose eyes are fixed on us, I realize the night's not over yet and there's something else we have to do.

"Don't freak out, okay?" I say softly, moving closer to her.

She arches an eyebrow, watching me curiously. When I place a hand on her cheek, her breath hitches. My eyes lock onto hers, and not for the first time, I wonder how they can be that pretty. They're just eyes, but they draw me in.

My throat dries. "Remember when we talked about the terms of this arrangement and you mentioned a kiss or two?" I don't wait for her reply. "This is the first one."

Her eyes widen, and instead of waiting for her to fully understand what I'm saying, I dip my head and brush my mouth over hers. Her body is still a little stiff, but when she parts her lips on a sharp inhale, I taste something sweet and minty at the same time. My blood thrums.

What I meant to just be a quick kiss for her parents turns into something more. Her mouth is warm and soft and I can't resist another taste. And another. She responds to me, wrapping her arms around my neck. My hands slide up to her hair and I get the overwhelming urge to deepen the kiss, to wrap my fist around her hair and pull until her mouth opens fully for me. Until I can take everything she has to give.

My heart starts to pound. I'm about to tilt Astoria's chin up even more when the sound of a throat clearing reaches through the haze in my mind. We jerk apart suddenly like someone fired a gun. I don't even look at her, instead turning in the direction of her parents. Her mom is beaming; her dad just looks annoyed.

"Good night, Carlo," he calls loudly.

I nod, about to head into my car, but I manage to sneak one more glance at her. Her dark hair is mussed from where I was pulling on it and her lips are swollen. The sight evokes something visceral in me, hot and possessive. I grit my teeth and try to shake it off.

"I'll call you, okay?"

Astoria nods but she can't seem to make eye contact. Not that I blame her. I step into my car and drive away from the Bianchi mansion.

Mission accomplished. But why does it feel like I just changed the rules of the game?

I'M EXHAUSTED as I walk into my apartment building, taking the elevator up to the fifth floor. I barely pay any attention to my surrounding as I open the door to my home mechanically. My mind is elsewhere as I remove my jacket and undo the first few buttons of my shirt. The lights in the apartment suddenly flicker on. I barely register surprise before my hand closes around my gun and I point it in the direction of the body in the room.

Christian grins. "Nice reflexes, *fratello.*"

I blow out a breath before placing the gun back into the back of my shirt. "What the fuck, Chris? I didn't give you a key so you could sneak up on me like that."

"No, you gave it to me so I could let myself in whenever I wanted. Which I did," he states, dropping the remote that controls all the lights back on the table. He walks over to me, his eyebrows raised. "Why were you so lost in thought?"

"No reason," I mutter, sinking onto the couch.

I rub my forehead slightly, feeling a headache creeping in. Christian's still standing, watching me curiously. "Where were you?"

"With Khalil," I reply.

While he and Christian have never met in an official capacity, he knows of him and vice versa.

"Really? I thought you'd be with Astoria Bianchi."

I hate the way my body reacts to the sound of her name. I haven't seen Astoria in over a week. We've exchanged a few texts, but they were light and straight to the point. It's pretty clear we're avoiding each other, which is honestly the right thing to do. Because I have no idea how I'd act in her presence.

"So?" Chrisitan prods and I look at him, eyebrows raised. "How are things going with her?"

"Fine," I reply.

My eyes flutter shut as the pain in my head increases. I don't open them even when I feel him take a seat beside me on the couch.

"You know, when I said we had to acquire the building at all costs, this wasn't what I had in mind."

"Mmm."

"You don't even know her. And you don't like most people. In your words, you prefer to keep human contact to a minimum. I'm just saying, maybe this is a bad idea."

I make another non-committal hum. He already said all this when I told him my plan, but leave it to my brother to continuously reiterate his arguments whenever something happens that isn't within his control.

"Come on, Lo. Are you even listening to me? What if Salvador finds out? He might be a good man, but we both know how he has treated those who have crossed him in the past. He wasn't best friends with *Papa* for no reason."

"He won't find out," I say, my eyes still closed.

"I still think it's a bad idea."

"I know. Now go. Don't you have a wife to go bother?" I ask. It's been a long day and I'm exhausted.

"She's pissed at me. Why do you think I'm here? She kicked me out of the house."

"What did you do?"

"I bought one of her paintings behind her back. It didn't sell at the last art show and she seemed upset, so I asked someone to purchase it for me."

"I fail to see how that's a problem."

"Exactly!" Christian exclaims. "But apparently, me buying it behind her back was deceitful and she wanted to sell it because someone loved it, not because her husband was pitying her."

I scoff. "That's ridiculous. I'm sure you didn't buy it

because of pity but to make her happy. Then again, I don't understand your relationship, or any relationships at all. Just suck it up, brother. Buy her flowers or something and she'll get over it."

"You're just saying what you think I want to hear." He sighs. "I should have gone to Toph. You're no help."

My eyes flutter shut again. "Mmm," I say, back to giving non-committal responses.

"Seriously, instead of this farce of a relationship, haven't you at least considered a real one? What about Cara?"

"Christian, I love you, I really do. But just shut up for a while, okay?"

He falls silent. For all of ten seconds.

"You okay?"

"No," I say, groaning. "My head fucking hurts."

"What happened?"

"There was a confrontation at the casino. I defused it, but one of the drunk bastards hit me over the head with a chair. I was fine earlier but it's really starting to screw with me."

"Shit. Should I get you some drugs?" Christian asks, concern bleeding into his tone.

"No, I'm fine. Just go home, okay?'

"You sure?"

I nod. "I'll just take some aspirin and sleep."

He gets to his feet, and I feel him linger for a few more seconds before he heads for the door. Silence fills the apartment when I hear it close. I'm glad it was him here. He's the only member of my family that would have heeded my request. Mom would have fussed over me, Topher would have been an annoying twat. But Christian always understands when I need to be left alone. Which is almost always.

I manage to take a shower and reheat some leftovers.

After dinner and some drugs, the headache lessens. My phone pings with a text as I head to bed.

> Astoria: Hey.

Nothing else, just hey. I should sleep but I want to know what she wants.

> Me: Hey.

Two can play at that game.

> Astoria: How are you?

Now I'm really curious about what she needs.

> Me: A woman of many words. I'm fine. Just got back from work. You?

> Astoria: I'm still at work. It's a Tuesday.

> Me: Right. How's Sarah?

> Astoria: She's better. I'm thinking of discharging her soon.

> Me: That's good. The kid should go back to school.

> Astoria: Do you want to meet her? You seem curious. You're always asking about her.

I consider that for a moment. Do I really want to meet a patient of hers? Not exactly, but the conversation I happened to overhear has never really strayed from my mind.

Me: I'm not sure that's a good idea.

Astoria: But Sarah wants to meet you too. I've told her all about you.

Me: You told your adolescent patient about your fake boyfriend?

Astoria: Yes. Her and her mother.

I sigh softly.

Me: Fine. I'll come to the hospital tomorrow.

Astoria: Okay, great. See you then.

Me: Is that why you texted?

Astoria: Something like that.

I only allow myself a moment of hesitation before texting back.

Me: If I didn't know better, I'd think you missed me.

Astoria: Good thing you know better.

I grin.

Me: Good night, dolcezza.

Astoria: Night.

Weirdly enough, by the time I place my phone on the bedside table, my headache's pretty much cleared, and I manage to fall asleep easily. Astoria's face is at the forefront of my mind as I do so. I guess that explains why I dream about her.

By the time I wake up the next morning, all I have is the memory of her smile. The dream is already receding from my brain, but I'm irritated regardless. Fuck, she's really messing with me.

The men notice I'm snippier and Christian raises an eyebrow.

"What's up with you?" he questions.

"Nothing."

"Really? Because you seem pissed. How's the headache?"

"Gone," I tell him.

"If you're still in pain, you'd better go get it checked out at a hospital."

"Christian, I'm fine," I assure him.

I don't think it's worth mentioning that I'm already planning on going to a hospital. It's not like I'm going there for a checkup. Plus, I'm really not in pain anymore. Christian seems appeased and he moves on to our topic of discussion.

"You think the Santos are planning something?" I ask my brother.

We've noticed some uprisings among members of our outfit. Small things, like carving out territory and staking claim to profits that aren't theirs. Desantos used to be an independent group until Christian cut their leader a deal. Instead of rightfully wiping them out, we absorbed them into our family. The convergence was seamless and for the past few years, things have been pretty quiet. But Romano Santos seems to be biting off more than he can chew at the moment and it's getting worrisome.

Christian's jaw tightens. "It's pissing me off. We're facing problem upon problem. James Malone, Romano Santos. Hell, even Salvador Bianchi."

"Calm down, Chris," I tell him. But I can understand his aggravation.

"We're hitting opposition within our ranks, Carlo. To the outside, it might not seem like much, but it could blow over at any time."

"I'll take care of Romano," I say, but Christian shakes his head.

"No, you already have a lot on your plate. I need you to focus on Bianchi. I'll take care of Romano. And while I hate to bring Topher into this, he and Kat are going to have to help us with her dad. He needs to lay off us. It's time we made peace."

"James Malone is a stubborn, prideful man with an over-inflated ego and a strong sense of justice. We're a mafia organization. I doubt he has any plans to make peace."

"Sure, but we're going to use his daughter and granddaughter to get to him. Emotional blackmail," Christian says, a glint in his eyes.

I shrug. I'm sure he'll handle it. Like he said, I need to focus on the Bianchis. I get a text from Astoria a few minutes after leaving the office, asking if I'm on my way. A part of me isn't ready to face her yet, but like my brother said, I need to focus on getting the building. So I head over to the hospital, hoping whatever it is that's fucking with my head will eventually go away.

# CHAPTER 9
*Tori*

I must have run over the kiss a million times in my head —the way it felt, the way I reacted to it, the feeling of his hands on mine. But eventually, I've reached a point where I berate myself for even thinking about it at all. He kissed me because my parents were there. To make our relationship seem real. That's all it was. The fact that I liked it—a lot—is inconsequential.

My mind returns to the present and I try to concentrate on the book in front of me. But a sharp knock at the door to my office causes me to immediately sit upright. I call for the person to come in and the door opens.

Carlo's standing there.

I get to my feet, slowly taking in his outfit—a crisp black button-down and dark jeans. I stand in front of him for a moment, torn about how to greet him.

Should we hug? Then again, there's no one else here and everything we do is for show. Right?

He doesn't make a move toward me so I stay put and I stare at him.

"You look different," I state for a lack of anything better to say.

He makes a small noise of agreement. "I don't always look like... what did you call it? A sulky mafia boss?"

I smile. "Unfortunately, you still look like one. It's your aura."

"Might need to work on that," he muses.

The air between us is a little awkward but since he seems intent on ignoring it, I roll with it. After all, he decided to cut off the lines of communication for a week in order to draw a clear line. I'm perfectly capable of taking a hint.

I clear my throat. "So..."

Carlo arches an amused eyebrow. "So? What's up with you, Tori?"

"Nothing," I say quickly. "I'm perfectly fine."

"Alright. Are you going to take me to the kid or not?"

I inwardly sigh. He's perfectly composed. I wish I was half as adept at compartmentalizing my emotions. You never know what he's thinking. It's such a nice ability to have.

"Sure, let's go meet her. Although she might not be completely receptive."

"Why not?"

I look away. "I might have spent the week complaining about what an ass you are."

He rolls his eyes. "I am not an ass." I shrug. He sighs. "Fine. Hopefully the gift makes up for it."

My eyes widen. "You brought something? That's so..." I cut myself off because I have a feeling Carlo D'Angelo would not like being referred to as sweet.

For the first time, I notice he's holding a small bag. He holds it out and reaches inside for a box of chocolates. My heart melts.

"Oh," I manage.

"Yeah. I figured I'd bring the kid a present. You think chocolates are okay? I wasn't really sure what to get for her." He looks a little out of place.

Damn, I never thought I'd see this. He seems nervous. It's adorable. Another adjective I doubt he'd like being used in relation to him.

I quickly shake my head. "There's no need, Carlo. It's a pretty big box," I say, smiling.

"You sure?"

"Yeah. I'm sure she'll love it."

He looks like he's about to bring up something else, so I quickly link my arm through his and lead him out of the office. I ignore how nice his arm feels, big and strong. His muscles are practically flexing with every move.

A soft, silent sigh escapes me. In hindsight, I probably should have chosen a fake boyfriend that was less sexy.

I clear my throat as we enter the ward. There are six hospital beds in here and three of them are currently occupied. The parents of the other two kids are with them, curtains drawn around them to provide privacy. We walk toward Sarah's bed. Her parents aren't here right now but her mom has been a part of our conversations, and they knew we were stopping by.

"Doctor Tori!" Sarah beams. She's much better than she was a week ago. Her vitals are great and she's not in any pain anymore.

"Hi, sweetie. How are you?"

"Fine," she says quickly. She looks pointedly at Carlo. "Is he your boyfriend?"

I have to practically pull him forward. "Yeah. Sarah, meet Carlo. Carlo, Sarah," I introduce.

Carlo dutifully offers his hand to the little girl for a shake. She blushes as she obliges.

"Hi, Sarah," he greets.

"You're really handsome." She giggles.

Now it's my turn to blush. It turns out adolescent girls don't really have filters.

"Thanks," Carlo says, amused. "You're not so bad yourself."

She blushes even harder, her face turning red. "Thank you. Oh, I'm not supposed to like you, though."

"Oh, really?" Carlo smirks. "Why?"

"Because you made Doctor Tori sad."

"I did?"

"Yeah. She said you had a fight and then you wouldn't talk to her. I think she missed you."

"She did, huh?" Carlo asks, sounding pleased.

His gaze on my face is practically searing but I don't look at him. I instead glare at the little demon on the bed.

"I never said that," I state.

Sarah shrugs. "Yes, but you came in here with a tub of ice cream and kept talking about how upset you were because you got into an argument, so I put two and two together."

Carlo's laughing now. I want to disappear.

Okay, so maybe I was a little upset. We had a small argument and then he kissed me and then he vanished. The next day, I was in the mood for ice cream. Sarah might be nine but she's also good company. I'm really going to miss her when she's discharged.

"Ok Ms. smarty pants, no more secrets for you," I say, jokingly.

"Don't listen to her," Carlo says, still smiling. "Here. I have something for you."

He hands her the box of chocolates and all my annoyance vanishes at the priceless look on her face. Big blue eyes tear up as she stares down at her gift.

"You got this for me?"

Carlo nods.

"Thank you."

"No problem. I just wanted to help you feel better. Don't cry," he says, sounding completely discomfited by the sight.

Thankfully, Sarah doesn't cry, but she does sit up and throw her arms around Carlo's midriff. He stiffens a little but manages to relax enough to pat her head. It's all so cute, I wish I could take a picture.

"I think it's perfect that you're dating Doctor Tori," Sarah says, looking up at him.

"Oh yeah?" Carlo asks.

She nods enthusiastically. "Yes."

"You little minx. You switched up so fast over a box of chocolates," I say jokingly.

She ignores me. "You can't break up with Doctor Tori, okay? Promise me. And promise me you won't fight with her again."

She even holds out her pinky for effect. Carlo looks at me, and something flickers in his expression. Then he looks back at the little girl and links their pinky fingers.

"I promise."

Adults are awesome at making promises they can't keep. Sarah asks him a couple more questions and then we have to leave. Carlo follows me back to my office. Most residents don't have offices, but owing to the shortage in pediatric doctors, I was lucky to get one.

Carlo's eyes sweep over the mess on the table as he takes a seat in front of it. I'm immediately self-conscious, moving to arrange some of the books and the files.

"I do a lot of research," I mutter.

"I didn't say anything, *dolcezza,*" he says, amused.

"You were judging." I grab the book I was reading earlier before sitting down. "So, what'd you think of Sarah?"

"I think you spend way too much time talking to little kids," he states. "But she's a cute kid. How about her parents?"

"They're pretty busy. They own a fast-food restaurant. It's the family's only source of income so they have to be there a lot. It's why I spend so much time with Sarah, so she doesn't get lonely. Her parents are trying the best they can."

"Alright." He nods. "What time do you get off work?"

"In about thirty minutes. Why?"

"I was going to take you home."

"Oh, right," I say, laughing nervously. "About that..."

He arches an eyebrow as I trail off. "Spit it out, Astoria."

"The reason I texted you yesterday was because my parents, um, pointed out something in relation to our fake relationship."

"What?" he asks, his gaze turning sharp.

I'm sure my cheeks are bright red as I explain, "Well, they got suspicious because I'm still getting home around the same time every night and I'm spending all my nights at home so they're curious about when we actually spend time together. My mom asked me point-blank why I haven't been spending much time with you. So, basically, I think it's best if I don't go home tonight so they think we're bonding."

Carlo doesn't say anything. As always, his expression gives away nothing. Finally, after several seconds, he speaks.

"Right. I never actually thought about that."

"Me either. It's not like we have a manual on how to fake-date. But yeah, it's a pretty big oversight," I say, biting on a fingernail. "I actually considered going to sleep at a friend's house instead of asking you but I was worried it would somehow get out and everything would be ruined."

"Astoria, it's alright," Carlo states. "Sure, you can stay over at my place. There are two bedrooms, but the guest bedroom doesn't have a bed in it. You can have my bed, though, and I'll sleep on the couch."

My cheeks heat. "I'm so sorry. I don't mean to bother you."

"Hey," he says, his eyes meeting mine, "this is as much my problem as it is yours. We're in this together, okay?"

I nod. "Yeah. Thank you."

"So you can finish reading or whatever it is you're doing and then we can go."

"Alright."

He leans back in his chair and pulls out his phone while I try to focus on the textbook in my hands. But I'm distracted. He's too close and my eyes keep straying in his general direction. Eventually, I give up and get to my feet.

"Let's just go," I announce, moving to take off my lab coat.

Carlo doesn't say a word as I gather my bag and other essentials. When I'm done, he gets to his feet. We're about to walk out when someone barges in without knocking. Blue eyes widen in surprise.

"Sorry, Tori. I should have knocked," Nora says apologetically as she looks from me to Carlo.

I sigh. "It's fine. What's up?"

Her eyes stray to Carlo. She offers him a small smile. "Hey, you probably don't remember me, but we met a while ago. I gave you directions to Astoria's office?"

Carlo's tone is bland. "Sure. Nice to see you again."

Nora turns to me again. She's still in her nursing scrubs and there are dark shadows under her eyes. I'm guessing she had a shift in the ER and is exhausted. Nora's the only true friend I've managed to make since I started working here. But we're both so busy, we barely have time to talk.

"Wait, he's really your boyfriend? I meant to ask but it's been a crazy week," she says.

I hesitate. I could tell her the truth. It would mean one less person to keep up this ruse around. But it's risky, and I'm sure Carlo would disapprove.

"Yeah. I meant to tell you. Carlo and I started dating recently."

There's a flicker of hurt in Nora's blue eyes. "Oh, how recent?"

"About three weeks ago. I'm really sorry, Nora. I should have told you but we've been…"

"Busy. Yeah, I know. Anyway, it's nice to meet you, Tori's boyfriend," she says, facing Carlo. Her tone is a little unkind.

"Carlo," he corrects. "And you are?"

"Nora. I'm Tori's friend. I'm sure she's mentioned me."

There's some animosity in their interaction, so I quickly butt in before things escalate. Nora's confrontational and highly suspicious. I have no doubt she'll start shooting question after question if I let her.

"We were just going to leave, Nora. What did you need?"

"I was going to ask for a ride home so we could talk but I'm guessing that's out of the question," she says, eyeing Carlo.

"Yeah, I'm sorry. We'll talk tomorrow, I promise."

"Okay. Bye, Tori." She hugs me briefly before walking away.

"I don't think she likes me very much," Carlo notes.

"I wonder why," I say dryly.

He smirks before placing a hand on my waist to lead me

away. The touch is light and thrilling at the same time. I couldn't remember the last time I wanted a guy's touch, but Carlo seems to be great at eliciting feelings I once thought dormant.

Our kiss flows back to the forefront of my mind and my body brims with electricity. He thankfully doesn't notice, too focused on guiding us toward the elevator. He presses the button for the first floor. Being in an enclosed place with him is suffocating and I can't get out fast enough.

We head for the parking lot, and I'm already dreading the night we'll have to spend together. But Carlo's the epitome of professional. Even if I'm entertaining insane stupid thoughts, I can count on him to keep his head on his shoulders.

The drive is quiet until I start to feel like I'm about to break out in hives.

"You were pretty good with Sarah today. Have you ever thought about having kids?" I ask to fill the silence. "Or is that sorely in the realm of none-of-my-business?"

Bitterly, I remember the way he dismissed my innocent question about his father. He could have told me he wasn't comfortable talking about it. Instead, he clammed up and dismissed me. I had forgotten about it but now I'm annoyed again.

"I was wondering when you'd bring that up," Carlo says.

"You mean, you being a total asshole?"

To my irritation, he smiles. "I'm sorry for shutting you down like that," he says in the most unapologetic tone ever.

My eyes narrow. "You're not very good at this apology thing, are you?"

"Nope."

My lips twitch. Honestly, I'm over what happened. A conversation with Sarah and a tub of ice cream helped, but still... I wish he hadn't shut me down. Then again, he doesn't owe me anything. I said I wanted us to be friends, but he's never expressed a similar sentiment.

"I adore my nieces and nephew. They're the most precious things in the world to me. And I've never had an aversion to kids," Carlo starts. My eyes cut to the side of his face and I realize he's actually opening up. "But I've also never spent much time wondering if I'd ever have them."

"Why not?" I question.

"Well, first off, it's not really up to me. I wouldn't be the one pregnant. I guess if my significant other wanted kids, I wouldn't have an objection to it," he informs me, and I'm immediately blown away. Every time I think I have him all figured out, he surprises me. "I'd have to find a significant other first, though. And the odds aren't in my favor."

"What? There aren't tons of women clamoring for the attention of Mr. Sulky Mafia Boss himself?" I joke.

He chuckles. "I've been told I don't have the best personality. Plus, most women tend to get turned off by all the murder."

"I doubt that's true. You're so much more than that."

Carlo briefly turns to look at me. An emotion I don't understand flashes in his eyes.

"You just have to put yourself out there, Carlo. I'm sure you'd be surprised just how many people would be willing to know you."

# CHAPTER 10

*Carlo*

Astoria smells like lavender and strawberries. Noticing her scent or being hyperaware of it isn't something I anticipated, but now that I have, it's all I can think about. It's intoxicating, almost like I could get drunk on it.

She's quiet as I lead her into the apartment. I try to see the place through her eyes. Like I told her, my mom picked out all the furniture. Some of the art pieces hanging on the wall are Daniella's. I purchased them to make her happy, not because I really gave a fuck. Astoria smiles slightly as she takes it all in.

"It looks like a typical bachelor pad," she says.

I'm not sure if that's a good thing or a bad thing. I don't ask. "Right. So what do you need? Are you hungry?"

She shakes her head. "No, just exhausted. It's been a long day."

I completely agree. "Alright, then. Sleep."

She follows as we cross the marble floors to my bedroom. I'm not used to people being in here, but I ignore the slight discomfort. Our arrangement is beneficial to me and I'm going to have to suck it up.

I gesture at the black door. "That leads to the bathroom. Is there anything you need?"

She considers it and then hesitates. I wait for her to speak.

"Maybe something to change into? I'm sorry, I should have thought this through a little better. I didn't pack anything."

I huff out a breath. "It's fine." I head into my closet and pull out a black shirt. "Here, you can change into this. I think we should take turns getting ready for bed. You can go first."

I exit the room without a backward glance, heading into the living room. I grab extra blankets for myself and fashion a makeshift bed on my couch. My mouth curls in distaste as I stare down at it. I'm half-tempted to ask Astoria if we can share my bed, but I don't trust myself to do that. Even the thought of sleeping next to her makes my blood thrum.

On some level, I understand that being attracted to her is normal. She's beautiful and so fucking smart. That doesn't mean I'm not berating myself with every look and every indecent thought. This is purely business.

When she steps outside of the room ten minutes later, though, it becomes impossible to remember how to be professional. My mouth dries as I stare at her. Her dark hair is down, curly strands billowing behind her.

She's wearing my shirt, which is so large it practically swallows her and stops at the middle of her thigh. I never thought I'd get off on seeing something as simple as my clothes on another woman. She shuffles on her feet and my eyes are immediately drawn to the awkward look on her face. I've been staring too long.

Without a word, I head into the room, deciding a shower might be in order. I strip out of my clothes. My muscles are tense and her proximity's really fucking with my head. By the time I'm done, my head's much clearer. I put on some shorts and a black tank before heading back out.

I don't immediately make my presence known, choosing to watch as Astoria walks around the living room. When she stops in front of a glass showcase containing some of my more prized possessions, I stiffen. There's a hidden compartment holding all of my guns that she shouldn't be able to see. It's something else that catches her eye. She reaches for a small wooden box and has barely opened it before I'm ripping it out of her hands.

She lets out a small squeal of surprise, whirling around to face me.

"Don't touch that," I say, my voice coming out sharper than I intended. I reach over to place the box back.

Astoria blanches. "I'm so sorry. I didn't realize it was…" She tapers off.

I take a deep breath, rubbing an aggravated hand over my face. I'm on edge.

"No, I'm sorry for snapping."

She nods and I'm suddenly acutely aware of our closeness. She's right in front of me, and now her scent is starting to needle my senses. I take a step back, then another.

"I am so sorry," Astoria says again.

"It's fine, Tori."

"Not just that. I mean for everything. You had to give up your bed and I'm here and I'm touching your stuff. I'm just sorry we're in this situation."

"It's not your fault, *dolcezza*."

"Actually, it kind of is," she mutters. "Anyway, I'm going to bed now. Good night, Carlo."

She starts toward the door.

"It was my father's."

She immediately stills but she doesn't turn around.

"The thing in the box belonged to my dad. That's why I —" I stop talking. I've already revealed much more than I'm comfortable with.

"I understand."

I release a slow breath. "Good night, Tori."

She walks into the bedroom and I'm left alone. I rub the back of my neck, letting out a frustrated breath. It's going to be a long night.

---

I WAKE up to the sound of soft cries. My eyebrows furrow as I sit up and check the time. It's 2am. I've only been asleep for two hours. When the cries turn into quiet screams, I bolt up and immediately head for my bedroom. I hurriedly open the door.

Astoria's in the middle of the bed. Ice immediately floods my body at the sight of her. She's shifting uneasily in her sleep, soft cries as she begs someone not to touch her. My hands fists at my sides as I approach the bed. Tiny shivers are racking her body and her breathing is erratic. I need to wake her up but I'm not sure how to go about it. I climb onto the bed, sitting beside her and placing my hand on her cheek.

"Astoria," I say gently.

"Please," she cries.

"Come back to me. Come on," I urge.

I thumb away a tear from her eyes before calling her name again. This time, her eyes open. She shivers before blinking once, staring at me. Several moments pass before she jerks upright, looking around in fear.

"Oh, god," she says, horrified.

"Hey, it's okay." I pull her closer until she's in my lap and I'm stroking her hair.

I hold her tight until her body stops shaking and I'm sure she's calm. Astoria lifts her head, hazel eyes staring into mine. I really hate looking into her eyes, because sometimes it feels like I'll never be able to stop. I lift my hand and gently wipe away some of her tears.

She doesn't say a word but I notice her cheeks slowly reddening. She pulls out of my embrace, shifting until there's space between us on the bed.

She opens her mouth, "I am so—"

"Don't apologize," I cut in sharply. "Tell me who hurt you."

My jaw tightens as I remember the sound of her cries. I want nothing more than to hunt down the architect of her suffering and put a bullet in their head. Astoria's expression flickers between dread and mortification.

"Astoria…" I prompt.

She shuts her eyes briefly. "You weren't supposed to hear me. I-I didn't know I was going to have a nightmare."

"That wasn't a nightmare," I correct sharply. "Something happened."

"It's been so long," she says helplessly. "I haven't had a nightmare in forever. I think it's-it's probably because I'm sleeping somewhere unfamiliar. I told you, I don't like change. My brain's hardwired to feel comfortable in certain places, and when I wasn't, it must have unlocked memories I've repressed and I wasn't—that wasn't supposed to happen."

The sight of her struggling and feeling bad about something that she obviously has no control over causes my jaw to clench.

"Tell me what happened," I ask again.

She sucks in a breath before raising her hand and biting down on a fingernail. I shift closer and run my hand through her hair.

"I know it's asking a lot to trust me but I'd never hurt you, Tori. I swear it. I just want to know what happened. Please."

"It's not—" She falters. "It's not something I can just talk about."

I try to convey just how much I want to be here for her. To help her or at the very least, put a bullet in the perpetrator's head. She looks into my eyes searching for something. Finally, she sighs. I watch as she sucks in a deep breath before seemingly steeling herself. Her voice is low and detached as she speaks.

"I was_" she pauses for a moment.

I realize how uncomfortable she is. "Actually, maybe you can tell me some other time and I promise if I can help you, I will. You want to... watch a movie or something?" I ask trying to change the subject. .

"I was sexually assaulted in my junior year of college."

I suck in a sharp breath but don't speak, letting her continue. Although a murderous rage fills me and I find myself counting to ten in my head so I don't fly off the handle.

Astoria's eyes take on a faraway look like she's trying hard not to think about it. "It's ok Tori, we can talk about it another time, I don't want to fuck your night with my questions."

"No, I ummm... I was drugged at a party by my date. He gave me something that knocked out my body although I was still very aware of what was going on. He got me into a bedroom and then h-he took my clothes off and started..."

Her eyes fall shut as a tear slides down. I wipe it away with my thumb. I'm still counting to ten in my head.

"He touched me everywhere, and the worst part is I was conscious. I was fully aware of everything he was doing against my will. I just couldn't stop him. Then he took off his clothes and he was going to rape me. He was extremely close but another guy walked into the room and he immediately knew what was going on. He tore him off me and stopped before things could go further."

"I'm glad you're ok. And it's not your fault you couldn't stop him. You may be beautiful, smart, and a pain in my ass but I'm sure he knew he was stronger than you or he wouldn't have tried that shit. What's his name?"

I ask, my voice eerily calm, despite the tornado of emotions rolling through me.

"Kyle Sanders," she whispers.

Kyle Sanders is a dead man.

"What the fuck happened to him?"

Astoria finally looks me in the eye. The blankness has receded a bit, like she's coming back.

"My dad's Salvador Bianchi. When he found out what happened, Sanders was locked up. He got tried and sentenced to four years in prison."

Outrage fills me at the paltry sentence and I begin to mentally calculate how long ago that was and if he's already out.

"You can stop making those serial killer eyes. Sanders died two years into his sentence. He was stabbed by another inmate. I like to think my dad had nothing to do with it but I'm also not ignorant or stupid. Dad was furious. I'm not happy that he died in prison though. Even though people like Kyle simply shouldn't exist, I believe in second chances," she says softly.

She's too damn sweet. I'm a little annoyed I'm not going to be able to dole out the proper punishment the bastard deserves. He should be tortured for days before finally meeting his maker. I would have loved to be his executioner. Especially now that I can see the effects of his actions on her. She's trying so hard to be brave.

I pull her closer and hold her. I'm not sure what to say or how to comfort her. This is new territory for me.

"I don't let what he did hang over me," Astoria says softly. "I was lucky. Really lucky, and I'm strong enough to push through every day without letting what happened affect me. It was hard at first, but I managed to find myself. And I live every day determined not to let Kyle Sanders have any impact on me. I don't even think about him. It was such a long time ago and I've moved on. Except for the nightmares."

I don't mention that it seems to me like she might just be repressing how she really feels about the situation instead of dealing with it outright. But she's already told me so much tonight and I don't want to push her any further. People have different ways of dealing with trauma.

I gently lift her chin so she's looking at me. "You're fucking brave, Tori. It's admirable how you've handled and continue to handle yourself. Just never let dirt like Sanders into your headspace. He's not worth your time."

She nods leaning against my chest. "I know," she says sleepily. "I'm scared to fall asleep. I don't want to dream again."

"You won't," I say assuredly. "Lie down, *dolcezza.*"

She does and before I can think better of it, I'm lying down beside her. I reach over to brush some of her hair from her face. For several seconds, neither of us breathes as we stare at each other.

"Sleep," I urge softly, breaking out of the spell her gaze casts.

She closes her eyes obediently and I finally get some

respite. I'm pretty sure I'm too on edge to fall asleep, but being so close to her, surrounded by her scent, is enough to lull me into slumber.

I wake up to sunlight and the smell of lavender and strawberries. Astoria's still fast asleep and somehow, while we slept, she's ended up with her head on my chest. I listen to her soft breathing for longer than I should be considered normal before slowly maneuvering her head off me and heading out of the room.

Last night shouldn't have happened. I never should have asked her to tell me about what happened to her. Because now every time I think about her, it's like there's a match being lit inside of me. A possessive urge to make sure that she's always safe. Whatever lines I've been trying to put in place have been practically incinerated.

With gritted teeth, I set to work preparing breakfast for the both of us. Astoria appears while I'm in the process of scrambling some eggs.

"Hey," she says softly, walking into the kitchen.

"Morning," I greet without looking up at her.

She doesn't say anything for a minute or two, just watches as I finish scrambling the eggs. When I move to set the small table in the kitchen, she takes the plates and does it for me.

We eat our breakfast in silence. The air is awkward and full of unspoken words, conversations we can't seem to get around to.

"Thank you for the meal. It was delicious," Astoria says when we're done.

"You're welcome."

She insists on doing the dishes, so I watch while leaning on the kitchen island. It's seven o'clock, but she mentioned yesterday that she doesn't have to go in to work until nine. Maybe earlier, if there's an emergency. When she finishes with the dishes, she dries her hand and comes to stand in front of me.

"So, I've been thinking…" she starts, biting her bottom lip nervously.

I wish she wouldn't do that. It's distracting, and now I'm thinking of her lips and how soft they were the last time, and how sweet she tasted. My cock twitches.

"And I definitely shouldn't have offloaded on you like that last night. I mean, this situation is already delicate enough. You didn't need to hear about my sob story. It's just… it has been a while since I _"

"Stop talking," I command. "Don't apologize for something someone else did. I absolutely needed to hear that, and now that I have, I'm going to make absolutely sure nothing like that ever happens to you again."

"But I—this isn't—" She stops, unable to properly articulate her words.

I move closer and grip her hand softly. Her head tilts back so she can look me in the eye.

"Don't apologize for it ever again. You did nothing wrong, okay?"

She nods once. My eyes narrow when she pulls her bottom lip between her teeth again. The urge to kiss her overrides every other thought. I realize how close we're standing and I want nothing more than to bridge the slight gap and press my lips to hers.

I don't know if it's something in my expression but Astoria's breath hitches and she shifts closer, open, inviting.

*Fuck it. What's one more taste?*

I lean in to capture her mouth in mine. But then the doorbell rings, forestalling our actions and wrenching us apart.

"Fuck," I say softly, glaring at my front door.

It rings again and I walk toward it, pausing to confirm

who's there. I curse under my breath when the cameras reveal who's standing on the other side. I swing it open to Khalil's completely unwelcome face. He raises a hand in salute.

"What's up, D'Angelo?"

"It's seven a.m. What are you doing here?" I question rudely.

He arches a dark eyebrow, seemingly amused. "I came to see my friend. What? Are you busy?"

I don't reply, my head filling up with scenarios where I strangle or choke him to death. Then his gaze travels behind me and his mouth curls up in a grin.

"Well, this is interesting."

Fucker.

# CHAPTER 11

*Tori*

I blink slowly as I take in the man who walks into the apartment. I don't miss the noise of protest Carlo makes or the resigned way with which he shuts the door. He frowns as the man makes his way over to me.

"Hi. Astoria, right?" he asks. "I'm Khalil. Carlo's friend."

Khalil's not as tall as Carlo. I estimate he's about six feet. His mouth is pulled into a charming, mischievous smile, and he has dark skin and clear black eyes. Objectively, I realize he's pretty attractive, with his squared jawline and broad shoulders. But my eyes stray to the man behind him and I'm more interested in why Carlo's jaw is clenched so tight.

I'm a little surprised but I find myself saying, "Funny, I didn't think Carlo was capable of making friends."

Khalil laughs. "Yeah, I definitely wasn't wrong about you."

"I'm sorry?"

"Khalil, shut up," Carlo says, stepping forward. He surreptitiously puts himself between me and his friend.

Said friend is visibly amused and seems to be enjoying

every moment of this situation. I'm even more curious about the dynamic between the two of them.

"Oh, stop being such a possessive twat. I was just talking to her." Khalil moves until he's standing beside me. "I've been meaning to meet you, actually. I'm very curious about Carlo's girlfriend."

"Well, it's nice to meet you," I say, glancing at Carlo and wondering just how much Khalil knows and if we're supposed to be acting like a loving couple right now.

"He knows," Carlo snarls, reading the look on my face accurately. "He knows the relationship is fake."

I look to Khalil, who shrugs innocently.

"What? I didn't do anything. But thanks for the reminder that she's single, Lo." He places a hand on my shoulder. "Come on, Ms. Bianchi. I want to know more about you. I heard you're a doctor, and I think doctors are pretty hot."

He starts to lead me away, but we've barely moved before Carlo's hand is clamping over Khalil's, which is currently wrapped around my shoulder. Carlo wrenches it away before once again placing himself between me and Khalil. I sigh, growing tired of the situation.

"Careful, Carlo. If I didn't know better, I'd think you were playing with fire," Khalil says.

I am so confused. What are they talking about?

"Astoria was just about to go get dressed," Carlo snaps.

"I was?"

He turns to look at me with a don't-fuck-with-me expression. I glare at him, but he's right. I'm only in his T-shirt, and it's not even semi-appropriate attire to be wearing in front of Khalil.

A voice in my head whispers that it's not appropriate attire for Carlo either, but I ignore it and start walking toward the bedroom. Carlo has pulled Khalil aside and their conversation has been reduced to hushed whispers. I cast one last glance at them before disappearing into the room.

Once inside, I sit on the bed and take a few moments to think about everything that's happened since I walked into this house yesterday. It's honestly a lot and I'm not sure where to even start unraveling it all. I'm not even sure I can. The entire time I spend getting dressed, all I can do is keep asking myself one question over and over again.

Before Khalil arrived, was Carlo about to kiss me?

Even if he was, it was probably in response to what he heard last night. The self-conscious part of my mind reasons that he likely sees me as someone to be pitied now. He was being uncharacteristically nice. Both last night and this morning. Maybe I'm just reading too much into everything. And even if he was about to kiss me, it would do me well to remember that we're in a fake relationship.

Things are already complicated enough.

When I exit the room, Carlo and Khalil are still speaking in whispers. They're in front of the windows, and I wait for a few seconds, hovering in the doorway. Then Carlo's eyes find mine and the thrum that rolls through my entire body is a clear sign that I might be fucked.

When did I start responding to him so instinctively?

He ends the conversation, moving over to stand in front of me. "You need to get to work, right?"

I nod once, watching the wheels turn in his head.

"I can't take you. Larsen and I have got business to take care of."

Khalil's still standing beside the large window, a slight smile on his face. I'm guessing Carlo threatened him in some manner because he doesn't even try to approach.

"That's fine. I can take a cab," I tell him.

It'll be great to have some time to think before I head to work.

"No," he says. "You can take my car."

My eyes widen. Carlo drives a black McLaren. Aren't men usually super possessive when it comes to their cars? Apparently not him because he doesn't even blink at the offer.

"But then—" I stammer, cutting myself off. "What would you drive?"

"I have another car, Astoria." He smiles. "Just take my car to work. I'll figure out how to get it back later."

"Okay. Thank you," I say gratefully.

He's been such a huge help. It occurs to me how far we've come in only a matter of weeks. When we met, he was cold and unrelenting. Now all I feel in his presence is warmth.

"Here are the keys. Drive safe."

Ah, there it is. Despite his unbothered front, it's hard for him to part with his car. His eyes simmer with unease. I smile as I accept the keys. I want to hug him, but I'm not sure that would be acceptable. The lines of our relationship are so blurred right now. How do you go from falling asleep in each other's arms to casual-acquaintances-slash-fake-boyfriend-and-girlfriend?

"I hope to see you again soon, Astoria," Khalil calls.

"You too."

I look at Carlo once more before heading for the door. I make sure to drive as carefully as possible as I head for the hospital. Despite how kind he's acting, I don't doubt Carlo would murder me if something happened to his car.

Okay, murder might be an exaggeration. I don't think he'd ever actually hurt me. But he'd definitely be pissed.

As soon as I arrive at the hospital, it's pretty clear it'll be one of those days. The days that make me love being a doctor. We're swamped with patients and I spend the first half of the day taking care of little kids with varying degrees of ailment. A broken foot, second-degree burns, cuts to be sewn up. I'm so consumed that I barely think about anything else. Finally, lunchtime rolls around and I get a break.

I practically drift across the hallways of the hospital. Until I'm accosted by a five-foot-three woman with blonde hair and blue eyes.

"Nora!" I yell when she pulls my arm.

"We're going to the cafeteria to get some coffee and food. And then we're going to talk."

I don't argue as she drags me there. She sits me down at an empty table before grabbing us some coffee. She returns to the table, blue eyes fierce.

"Drink," she orders.

I obediently gulp down some of my coffee.

"Now, tell me how it is you came about to be dating Carlo D'Angelo. Because I don't believe it for a second."

I open my mouth to tell her the story we fed our parents and then I shut it. With a small sigh, I ask, "How do you even know who he is?"

"His family's pretty notorious."

"Right," I say.

I always forget about the D'Angelos' popularity, which is not for the right reasons. I guess when you're in my world, you learn to be desensitized to that sort of thing. Before I knew Carlo, I judged him by what I had heard, as well. But he's so much more than that.

"Any reason you're supposedly dating a murderer?"

I wince. "Don't call him that."

Nora shrugs. "Hey, I'm just saying. You're a doctor.

Shouldn't it be against your code of ethics to even be associated with someone like that?"

"It's not that simple, Nora. Stop being so judgmental."

She murmurs something under her breath. "Well? I'm still waiting to hear how you two got together."

I really should start feeding her all the lies, but something stops me. I've never been great at making friends, and after what happened to me in college, I stopped trusting people altogether, keeping everyone at arm's length. But Nora and I have known each other for three years, and she has been nothing short of a good friend to me. She's dependable and fierce and I honestly need someone to talk to.

"It's not a real relationship," I confess.

Her mouth hangs open. "I'm sorry. What?"

I quickly explain my arrangement with Carlo and how it began. It takes a few minutes for Nora to comprehend my words, but then she's leaning back in her chair, shock evident on her face.

"Huh. It makes sense, actually. No way you're actually dating such a stuck-up man. And since you're not dating him, I can confidently say he's a rude ass. He seems intimidating and not your type."

"Well…." I trail off.

"What? Is he your type?" she questions, surprised.

I sigh. "I was getting to that bit. Things have been growing complicated."

"Define complicated," Nora prompts.

"Last night, we, uh, slept in the same bed together. And this morning after we had breakfast, I'm pretty sure he was about to kiss me. The lines are getting blurred and I'm not sure what's going on."

Nora's expression turns a little pitying. "Oh, sweetie, you

definitely should have come to me before getting into a fake relationship. Those are almost always doomed for failure."

"In what way?"

"I mean, it's pretty obvious you're already falling for him. I'm not sure what the neanderthal's intentions are"—I snort a little at the nickname—"but what I do know is that if you continue, you could get hurt. And I'd hate for you to get hurt."

I sigh softly and sip some of my coffee. "Maybe I'm reading into things that aren't actually there. I was pretty upset last night and Carlo comforted me. It was basic human decency. I doubt he has any feelings. He's always so professional when it comes to our arrangement."

Nora laughs. "Right, because sleeping next to you in the same bed is so professional."

"He didn't plan on it. It just sort of happened," I mutter.

"Listen, Tori. You know I think you're a woman of steel and strong as heck, but it kind of seems to me like he's got you wrapped around his finger. And I'd hate for him to exploit that."

"He won't," I say firmly. "I'm an adult, Nora. I can handle myself."

"You have feelings for your fake boyfriend," she argues.

"I *think* I have feelings for him," I correct. "It could just be hormones or pheromones and whatnot. I'm sure it's fine."

"It has been a long time since you had sex," Nora muses. "You think you're sexually frustrated?"

I laugh. "Maybe."

The conversation switches to something else and I enjoy the rest of my break in the company of someone I'm grateful to have in my life. Just before we leave the cafeteria, Nora places a hand on my shoulder.

"You can talk to me anytime, Tori. I'll listen and try to be less judgmental."

"Thanks."

"Also, don't get mad, but I'll also be freezing the ice cream until he eventually breaks your heart because I have a feeling he will and we'll be needing lots of it."

I roll my eyes. "You're being ridiculous."

"Oh, my sweet, sweet friend," Nora says, leaning to hug me. "Gotta go back to impending death."

I laugh as she walks off in the direction of the emergency room. It was definitely a good idea to tell her the truth. It feels like a weight's been lifted off me. At least I have someone I can depend on. Still, a part of me is worried. With what happened last night with Carlo and me trusting Nora with the truth, I'm worried that I'm losing all the cards I keep closest to my heart. They are suddenly in the perfect position to hit me where it hurts.

I manage to make it for another hour before I give in to something that's been niggling at me all day. Before I can stop myself, I grab my phone and text him.

> Me: Where are you?

He replies ten seconds later. I ignore the thrill that shoots through me as I read his response.

> Carlo: At work.

> Me: Okay. How do you plan to get your car?

> Carlo: I was going to come pick it up later.
> Maybe drop you off at home while I'm at it.
> What time do you get off?

Me: Eight-ish

Carlo: I might not be done by then. I've got a lot of shit to do.

Me: It's fine, Carlo. I have my own car. I can just drive it home and then you can come pick up your car here. I'll leave your key with the security guard.

Carlo: Still...

I try hard not to smile at his obvious hesitation.

Me: You're not my chauffeur, D'Angelo. I'm perfectly capable of driving myself home.

Carlo: Fine. I'll see you soon?

Me: Of course.

I drop my phone, ignoring the giddiness lighting up my insides. Sheesh, one would think I'm a teenager having her first crush.

By the end of the day, I'm ready to crawl into bed and not get up for several days. After making sure Carlo's car is sufficiently taken care of, I head home.

My mom's in the foyer when I arrive. She smiles brightly at me.

"Hey, sweetie. How was work?"

"Fine," I tell her.

"I see you didn't make it home last night. I know you were stopping by to hang out with Carlo but I didn't think you were going to stay the night. How were things at Carlo's house?"

I remember she's the reason I was even in the position I was last night and irritation flares through me. If she hadn't insisted I spend more time with him, I wouldn't have had that nightmare and told him everything. Then again, I have a feeling that's what brought us closer, so I can't really be mad. My mom's doing the best she can, encouraging me to chase what makes me happy. I'm glad she's so supportive.

"It was pretty good, Mom. He made me breakfast. He's actually a really good cook," I admit.

She laughs. "One would hope so. His mother and I used to be close and Martina's an abysmal cook. I'm sure Carlo had to pick up some things over the years."

"Oh, I hadn't realized you were close with his mom, too."

"I was. We were all friends but Carman's death changed everyone, I guess. Martina never really recovered. She drifted away and I haven't seen her since the funeral. Do you know where she is, *cara*?"

"Carlo told me she's in Milan visiting her sister."

"Oh. Well, I hope she comes back soon. It's likely we'll have a wedding to plan," my mom says excitedly.

"Let's not get ahead of ourselves," I remind her.

"Why not? The two of you make an amazing couple and honestly honey, you're not getting any younger. You have to start working on giving me grandchildren."

I swear if I have to hear her say that one more time.

"Which reminds me..." My mom trails off, going in search of something.

I wait patiently and when she returns, she's holding gold-embossed invitation cards.

"The Queens are planning an art exhibition. We're all invited. You should bring Carlo with you."

The event is a week away. I twirl the cards in my hand, wondering, hoping.

# CHAPTER 12

*Carlo*

"It's a stupid art show and we definitely don't have to go," Astoria says.

I chuckle as I grab something from the bedside table, making sure the phone stays placed against my ear.

"Dany happens to be one of the organizers of that stupid art show," I inform her.

She gasps. "Oh shit. I'm sorry, I had no idea."

"It's alright. She has a gallery of her own and she paints, as well. You might have noticed one or two of her paintings hanging on my walls."

"They were beautiful," Astoria murmurs.

"Yes, well, she's contributing to the art show, so I was always going to have to go. I thought about inviting you, actually, but it seems your mother beat me to the punch."

"Yeah. That's my mom, always racing to the finish line. She's already looking forward to our wedding."

"That's interesting," I drawl.

"More like terrifying." I hear the subtle doubt in her voice.

"Where's your head at, *dolcezza*?"

"Oh, it's nothing. I was just considering everything. We never explicitly stated an end date for our arrangement."

Her bringing up the fact that our relationship is fake effectively douses my good mood. But it also serves as a reminder not to get carried away. And especially not to spend the entire day thinking about her and the way she felt in my arms.

"I thought we agreed on keeping it up until we both got what we want."

"We did? Well, what if I'm not sure what I want?"

That's an interesting question. I'm not sure what she wants, either. This thing she's doing with me is temporary at best. If we ended things, her parents would one day be handing her yet another willing bachelor with a sizable inheritance. Doing this with me is a short-term solution for her.

"I'm sure you'll figure it out."

She hums softly.

"At least we have the *stupid* art show to look forward to," I say in a dry tone. "I have to go out of town tomorrow and I'll be gone for a few days."

"Oh, but you'll be back in time for the show?"

"Of course. I probably won't be able to see you until then."

I'm equal parts relieved and annoyed. Relieved because I'm fairly sure some time apart would do us some good, but a part of me doesn't want to be away from her. It's a conundrum. One I have no idea how to work around.

"It's fine. I'm sure I can survive a few days without seeing your broody face," she jokes.

"Very funny," I say dryly. "I have to go, okay? I'm really busy."

"Sure. I'd better get to bed. I'm exhausted. Good night, Lo."

My heart warms at her use of my nickname. If it were anyone else, I'd be warning them against it. Only family members and really close friends get to call me that. But Astoria's not just anyone. Not anymore.

I hang up the call and quickly get in a workout before going back to making some calls. Romano Santos made a move yesterday, and we have reason to believe he may be planning a gang war. Christian has me making calls to every single one of our associates to alert them to the situation. And tomorrow, I have to head to Connecticut to talk to a business partner.

This week is going to be long as fuck.

---

I GET BACK in town in time for the art show, but I've spent the past fifteen minutes sitting in my car, waiting for Astoria. She finally deems it fit to appear a few minutes later, looking like every man's dream. Her dark hair is in a bun atop her head with a few curls framing her face, and she's wearing a black dress that hugs her curves with a slit in front.

When she slides into the passenger seat of the car, the sight of all her exposed skin has me wanting to do something completely inappropriate. Instead, I force my gaze forward and clear my throat.

"What's your excuse this time, *dolcezza*? You're more than fifteen minutes late. And you can't use the fact that you're a doctor since you didn't go in to work today."

She grins as she looks at me. "The time got away from me."

I am not amused. I glare at her to convey that and she rolls her eyes.

"I haven't seen you in days. Don't be a grump."

Without another word, I pull out of the driveway of her parents' home, heading for the large silver gates.

"Your parents already left, right?" I ask.

She nods. "They got there an hour ago. Mom's head of some committee and had to get there early."

"You say that like it's a bad thing."

"It's unnecessary. Besides, it's fashionable to arrive late to events like this."

"I'm almost certain the person that made that rule was a kindred spirit of yours. Always tardy."

She throws me a look of indignation. Her phone goes off with a text and she smiles before replying. When it dings again, I decide I've exercised enough restraint.

"Who's texting you?" I ask, trying not to sound too sharp.

Her head swivels in my direction. "Oh, it's Nora."

"Your friend from the hospital?"

"Yeah, she was just talking to me about tonight. Which reminds me, I should probably tell you.."

"Tell me what?" I prompt.

"I told Nora the truth. About us."

Silence follows her announcement. I'm not sure how to take it.

"Are you mad?" Tori asks when I remain quiet.

"No," I inform her. "I'm just surprised you trust her that much."

"I'm surprised myself. But Nora's pretty awesome. I don't have a lot of friends. I'm usually so closed off. Not just because of what happened to me in college," she says hastily. "But I went through something pretty nasty in high school, as well."

"What happened?"

"My boyfriend cheated on me with my best friend at the

time. It felt like such a big slap in the face because I trusted them both. I guess since then I've just coasted through life waiting for everyone to betray me. But I'm ready to open up now. With Nora. And maybe even with you."

I stiffen. There's nothing inherently wrong with what she's saying, but the words veer into a direction we've both steadfastly tried to avoid for a week. Still, I'm not ready to face it right now. So I focus on the other part of her conversation.

"Sometimes, I truly despise people," I mutter. Astoria's eyes widen and I quickly clarify, "I'm talking about your fucktard of an ex and your former best friend. They're shitty people. Period."

She laughs. "Yeah, they are shitty people." She sobers up and I feel her gaze on the side of my face. "Are you sure you're not mad about me telling Nora?"

"Of course not. She's your friend and you trust her. I trust your judgment."

She seems appeased and we spend the rest of the drive in silence. We arrive at the art gallery and I realize I forgot one important detail. There's paparazzi here. Lots of them. Astoria must realize it at the same time because she stiffens.

"Um. We never talked about letting our fake relationship be so public," she says carefully.

I shrug, removing my seatbelt. "We might as well just roll with it."

I get out of the car and immediately walk over to her side to help her out. She links her arm through mine. Flashes of light and the click of cameras go off around us, but they leave ample space for us to cross into the venue. I tamp down my irritation. I really hate being in the public eye and this will keep me there for a while.

The only sign that Astoria's bothered by it all is her tight grip on my arm.

I turn to face her. "It'll be okay."

"You can't just blindly assure me about everything. You're not a superhero, Carlo. And there's no magical wand that you can wave to make everything okay."

"Hey, I'm hearing a lot of doubt when it comes to my abilities. I can do anything."

She sighs. "Except keep your ego in check."

My lips twitch but I don't smile. I lean closer to whisper in her ear. "Have I told you how beautiful you look tonight?"

She shivers slightly. "No, but I'd love to hear it."

"You're practically glowing, *dolcezza*."

I lightly graze the curve of her ear with my teeth to prove a point. She jerks slightly. When I pull away, her cheeks are tinged pink, and I smile in satisfaction.

We navigate the crowd, heading to where my brother and his wife are standing. Daniella beams at the sight of Astoria and hugs her like they're long-time friends. Tori seems a little uncomfortable, but as soon as Dany starts chatting her up about her dress, she relaxes.

"How was your trip?" Christian asks me.

I grit my teeth as I remember how terribly things went. "Don't ask."

"Well, I've got some good news. We might be able to contain Romano before an all-out gang war. He currently hiding out somewhere in Manhattan, but I know just how to draw him out."

"Good for you, brother," I tell him.

"Yeah. Things might be looking up. Malone also signed off on the release of our men that he had in custody."

"He did?" I ask warily.

"According to Topher, Katherine talked to him and they came to an understanding. He has promised to stop breathing down our necks and instead find something else to occupy his time. So long as we don't commit any crimes in his city."

"Well, how the hell are we going to do that? We run this city."

"Yeah well, we have to fall back and stay off the radar with the FBI for a while."

"I guess all that's left is to take care of Bianchi," I state, my gaze traveling to Astoria's parents at the end of the room.

They're surrounded by a group of people who are enthusiastically gesturing at the paintings. I'm much more concerned by the feeling of inadequacy in my gut. Christian's counting on me. I need to speed things up with the building.

Daniella leads us down the aisle, showing us the various paintings being displayed. I'm only half-listening. Astoria's sidled up beside me and when she intertwines our fingers, I don't object to the warmth of her hand in mine. I tell myself it's all for show, but I honestly don't know anymore.

My feelings are a jumbled-up mess.

I stumble to a stop when I recognize someone in front of us. Astoria stops as well, then Christian and Dany, who are behind us. The sight of Cara Oshiro has me gritting my teeth.

I haven't seen her in over a month. Not since the hotel. I've been trying to give her some space.

She offers me a nervous smile. Then her eyes drop to mine and Astoria's hands and her smile slips.

I understand how this must seem to her. I slowly unlace my fingers from Astoria and try to smile, although I'm sure it's more of a grimace. Technically, I don't owe her anything, but after the way our last encounter ended, it feels a little shitty of me to be throwing a new relationship in her face.

"Hey, Cara. Fancy seeing you here."

There's hurt in her expression as she looks at me. Her green eyes narrowed, she glances at Astoria before affixing me with a glare.

"Have I mentioned you're an asshole?"

This is a fucking mess.

# CHAPTER 13

*Tori*

S o this is her. The woman Carlo was in a relationship
with before he met me. She's beautiful, and while I
will never be that girl who compares herself to other
girls and demeans herself in the process, it's a little hard to
watch my "boyfriend" reunite with his ex.

And I'd be lying if I said it didn't hurt when he let go of
my hand like that. But I saw the expression on her face and I
have a feeling they didn't break up because feelings faded. He
probably doesn't realize it, but his eyes soften when he looks
at her. I've never seen him look like that before. Carlo doesn't
even notice as I inch backward and start walking away.

I hear the light clacking of heels behind me, and when I
turn, Daniella's there. She doesn't say anything, she simply
leads me to an empty hallway. I lean against the wall, trying
hard to stop picturing the look on Carlo's face as he looked at
Cara.

"Don't overthink it," Daniella says.

I look up as she brushes her red hair off her face. She has
been fairly nice to me all night, despite knowing that my relationship with Carlo is fake.

"What are you talking about?"

"Right now. You're overthinking what you just saw. Don't. If you overthink it, you'll start seeing things that aren't really there."

"I'm pretty sure I saw what was happening perfectly clearly."

She sighs and mutters to herself, "I really wasn't going to meddle this time."

"What are you talking about?"

"Listen, Tori, Carlo's a complicated man. I've known him for years and even I don't understand him. But I love him like a brother and I want him to be happy, which is why I'm going to advise you to be straightforward with him. He can be a little oblivious. If you want him to know something, you're going to have to literally shove it in his face."

I blink and stare and blink some more. "I have no idea what you're talking about."

She smiles. "I believe I was pretty clear. Take it from me, I was in a similar position with another D'Angelo brother. They can be dumb when it comes to how they feel. Sometimes they need a little push."

I sigh softly when I realize what she's insinuating. "No, Daniella. I don't—Carlo and I aren't…" I struggle to decide how best to explain our situation.

"I think you should talk to him about it," Daniella says softly. She offers me an encouraging look before straightening. "Right, well, I'm going to send him over here so you can talk."

I nod and she leaves. I turn over her advice in my mind. I'm pretty sure she just asked me to tell Carlo how I really feel. Only problem is, I'm not so sure myself. The only feeling that's clear right now is the jealousy that's threatening to explode in my gut.

It takes a few minutes before Carlo shows up. He walks over and I allow myself to admire him for a moment. He really is handsome. His face is the embodiment of the bad boy with a motorcycle your parents warn you away from in high school. But I can't imagine Carlo riding a motorcycle. He values order and control. He's wound up tight.

As always, his expression is carefully blank as he approaches, though I do catch slight worry flickering in the brown depths of his eyes.

"Hey, you okay?" he asks, his gaze roaming my face.

I let out a soft breath. And I decide to go into this rip-off-the-Band-Aid style. He stares at me curiously as I stand in front of him.

"Do you still love her?"

Carlo stares at me for several seconds, uncomprehending. When he finally gets it, his eyebrows furrow.

"No. I told you I've never been in love with anyone."

"But you dated her," I argue. "You care about her."

He looks uncomfortable now. "Cara and I never really dated. We were together but our relationship rarely passed the bounds of physical gratification."

I turn those words over in my head. "So… you were fuck buddies?"

Carlo makes a face. "In a sense, yeah."

"But you care about her," I prod.

He sighs. "Cara and I are complicated."

That does nothing to alleviate the feeling in my chest. The last thing I wanted was for him to refer to his relationship with her as "complicated." I wanted him to deny having any sort of relationship at all.

He must notice the expression on my face because his eyebrows crease. "What's going on in that head of yours?"

I swallow softly and look up at him. "If you and I weren't doing this... fake relationship, would you be with Cara?"

Now he seems even more uncomfortable. "I have no idea what you're talking about."

"You do," I say gently. "Just be honest. If you and I weren't fake dating, you'd be with Cara, wouldn't you?"

"Astoria." He sighs again.

That's it. He just sighs, but he doesn't give me an answer. My jaw clenches.

"Carlo, I need you to tell me the truth. Because if we're doing this and you—" I falter.

Carlo's staring at me. The look in his eyes is intense, and I have no idea what's going through his head right now. I take a deep breath.

"If I'm keeping you away from someone you have feelings for, then we need to stop. It's not right. You told me that you don't believe anyone could ever look past the surface and see the real you. Cara could be that for you. Don't let this fake relationship hold you back. I can't be the reason you're—"

"Astoria," Carlo cuts in. His hand slides up to my hair, fisting it. "Just shut up," he whispers and then his lips are on mine and every single thought evaporates.

The kiss is soft at first, sending shivers down my spine as his other hand moves down to my waist. His mouth gently teases mine open until my breath catches and I give him better access. My stomach clenches as his grip on my hair tightens. The kiss becomes deeper, rougher. My hands wrap around the back of his neck, bringing us closer.

*I could kiss him forever.*

Much too soon, though, the kiss ends, and Carlo pulls away abruptly. We're both breathing heavily. I look up at him but his eyes don't meet mine. He's looking at something behind me. Or someone.

"Mrs. Bianchi," he rumbles.

I jump away, turning to look at my mother. She's staring at both of us with wide eyes. My hand flies to my mouth when I realize she saw us.

"Mom! How long have you been standing there?"

She blinks. "Sorry, honey. I noticed Carlo walking over here and I was wondering if you were here, too. I just got here, promise."

"Oh," I say, relieved that she didn't hear our conversation. I quickly turn to Carlo and swallow softly. *Did he kiss me because he noticed my mom approaching?*

His expression gives nothing away. Disappointment pools in my gut. And hurt.

"I didn't mean to interrupt. I can leave."

"No, it's fine," I tell her. "Did you need me for something?"

"Yes, *cara*. A friend of mine wanted to meet you. It's fine, though. She can meet you later," my mom says, smiling.

"No, I can meet her now. I'll see you in there, Lo," I mumble without looking at him.

I just need to get out of here. I walk to my mom and lead her out.

---

THE REST of the night goes by and I'm barely present. I keep replaying the kiss and our conversation over and over in my head. More than anything, I hate how vague he was about his relationship with Cara. He didn't answer my questions, and it's even more annoying because more than anything, I've always known Carlo to be straight with me.

He's barely said anything to me, either. We've been drifting around the party, greeting acquaintances and pretending to be a loving couple. But I'm sure they must notice how stiff we're acting, especially me since my mind is miles away. I catch the worried glances Daniella throws my way, but she doesn't say anything. I'm glad Cara's not here anymore. I'm not sure how I'd act around her.

Finally, the exhibition ends and we can leave. Daniella gives me a hug before we step outside.

"If you need to talk, just hit me up, okay?" she tells me.

I nod, offering her a grateful smile. Then Carlo's leading me to his car. He doesn't immediately drive once we're inside. I count five breaths before he speaks.

"What's going on, Astoria?"

I glance at him. He's already looking at me, his jaw tense and a frown marring his lips.

"Not tonight, okay? I'm tired," I say on a sigh.

"Fine. But I'm taking you to my house," he announces.

"No!" I hurriedly say. "Take me to my parents' house."

"Astoria—"

"Carlo, I promise I'll talk to you when I'm ready. But I need some time alone right now."

He looks like he wants to argue but he refrains, looking away before starting the car. Then we're off. I usually hate long silences, but it's blissful as we drive.

When we arrive, I mumble out a goodbye before stepping out of the car. He drives away without another word. I can tell he's angry.

Good. I'm angry, too. But knowing him, his anger would be more controlled and we'd never get anywhere if we had an actual argument. He's not ready to be honest with me and I need some time away from him to sort out my thoughts.

I just need to know what's real or not.

My parents are having a conversation by the stairs when I walk in, and my mom raises a brow.

"I wasn't expecting you home tonight, *cara*. I thought you'd spend the night at Carlo's."

*Of course they did.*

"No, I decided to come home," I inform them.

My dad narrows his eyes. "Did you have a fight?"

He looks like he wants the answer to be yes. I can tell my dad is itching for a reason to disapprove of Carlo and end our relationship.

"Of course not, Daddy."

My mom slaps his stomach lightly. "Don't be silly, darling. They didn't have a fight."

"Then why didn't she hand out with him? They were partying it seems like a good night to hang out with the person you love and watch a movie or maybe go for a walk?" Dad shoots back.

I quickly look for an excuse. "Carlo had some work to do and I need to go in to the hospital early tomorrow," I lie.

My dad's brows furrow. "You never work on Sundays."

"Yes, but there's a patient I need to check on in the morning. Since Carlo's busy, I figured I'd just come home and go to the hospital on my own tomorrow."

"Hmm," is all he says.

My mom buys it, though. "That's fine, *cara*. It's late, you should go to bed."

I leave them at the stairs and head into my bedroom. As soon as I close the door, I fall onto my bed with a sigh. I wasn't kidding about being tired. Sleep is always my first reaction to anything stressful or problematic.

The last thing I see before I close my eyes is the look on Carlo's face as he stared at Cara. Something painful thuds in my chest and I can't help but wonder if I'm already doomed.

# CHAPTER 14

## *Carlo*

S weat clings to my forehead as my fist collides with the bean bag in front of me. My punches are measured, controlled, each one designed to land with just the right amount of force. My father always used to say there should be moderation in everything—even beating people up.

*Control and discipline.* Even now, he's still whispering in my ear. Everything I do, every action I take. I'm sure he would be so fucking proud of how well he's molded me.

My concentration breaks when I hear footsteps behind me. Then Topher waves his phone in my face, his mouth stretched into a wide smile. I stop punching the bag, breathing heavily as I turn to him.

"Have you seen this?" he questions excitedly, handing me his phone.

My eyes drift to the pictures. There's a light smile on Astoria's face as she stares at the cameras. Meanwhile, I'm standing beside her, my arms wrapped around her waist and my expression unflinching. I can't get over how right she looks there beside me.

***The Black Knight and the Bianchi Princess***

*Are Carlo D'Angelo and Astoria Bianchi New York's newest it-couple? At first glance, they might seem like an odd pairing, but the couple was simply stunning as they stepped out together last night at the Queens' exclusive art exhibition.*

The article goes on to explain how close we looked last night and how interesting it is that we started dating considering we've never been seen out in public before. I roll my eyes before handing back the phone.

"What? No comment?" Topher asks on a pout.

I shrug. "I was expecting it. I just wish they chose a less corny headline."

He chuckles. "I think you make a wonderful knight, *fratello.*"

"Fuck off," I say, my hand going to the scruff of my neck as I try to massage the tension there.

"You good?" Topher asks, staring at me curiously.

"Why do you ask?"

He smiles nervously. "I might have had a conversation with Dany before making my way here."

My jaw tightens. "One of these days, I'm going to have a conversation with our sister-in-law about proper boundaries and not telling everyone about my business."

"Easy, Lo. She only told me because she knew I was coming to see you."

"What exactly did she tell you?"

"Well, she said she was worried. Apparently, you and your *girlfriend* had a fight last night."

I roll my eyes. "We didn't have a fight."

"But something happened. Come on," he prods. "You can talk to me."

"There's nothing to talk about, Toph."

"Really? Because you seem like you need someone to talk to."

123

I glare at him. Even if I wanted to talk to someone, which I don't, he wouldn't be my first choice. I love my little brother, but Topher's not known for giving out the best advice.

I crack my knuckles as I think about the distant look on Astoria's face after our kiss yesterday. I realize she thinks I kissed her because her mom was there, and I also realize I should have immediately debunked that notion. But a part of me wants her to keep believing it.

I just hate that she's probably hurt and confused right now. I want to find her and tell her the truth, but I don't know what the truth is. Plus, she asked me to give her some space. We both need it right now. Maybe then I can get my senses in order.

"Fine. If you won't talk about Astoria, let's talk about Cara. I heard she was at the exhibition."

My glare intensifies but Topher doesn't let up.

"Before you say anything threatening, Cara's my employee. It's well within my rights to understand this situation so that I can ensure that my work environment continues to be manageable."

"That's complete bullshit."

"I'm serious," he says sagely. "An emotional, pissed-off woman is bad for business, Lo. Tell me what's going on."

I sigh because I know he won't let this go. "It's complicated."

Topher snorts. "Well, obviously. Seriously, Carlo, you need to work on your communication skills. I asked for an explanation and you gave me two words."

I ignore him, grabbing a towel to dab at the sweat on my face. Topher pinches the bridge of his nose in frustration.

"Come on, bro. Give me something. I'm curious. You and Cara have had something going on for a few years now. She doesn't talk about it and neither do you, but I know you both regularly get dirty in the sheets," he says, wiggling his eyebrows.

My lips twitch but I really want to hit him. *Dumbass.*

Topher continues, "Anyway, I always thought you'd eventually just suck it up and start dating her or something, but that didn't happen. Instead, you start dating Astoria—"

"Fake dating," I clarify, even though something tightens in my chest as I do so.

"Right, *fake dating*," he emphasizes. "But Daniella swears something else is going on between you and her, and now I'm confused about where you and Cara stand. Who do you actually have feelings for, *fratello*?"

He seems genuinely put out, and if it were any other topic of conversation, his expression would be funny. But I am not amused by his breakdown of my love life.

"That's for me to know, Toph, and for you to mind your own business."

Topher rubs his forehead on a groan. "If I'm this confused, I wonder how the women in question feel."

*Good point*, I admit grudgingly to myself. I don't say it out loud, though.

Topher's expression is serious as he stares at me. "Don't play with their feelings, Carlo. Don't string them along, either."

"I'm not," I say through gritted teeth.

Right now, I'm trying to make sense of the shit swirling around in my head. I have no idea what I want.

"Make the right decision," he continues.

"Would you quit it?" I mutter, getting annoyed.

He smiles. "I have to say, I'm really enjoying this. I haven't seen you this bothered over anything in, well... ever!" He laughs. "This is rich."

"Now that you're done pissing me off, you can go now," I say, pointing to the doors of the gym.

He's already cut into my workout time. I only do this a few times a week in the evenings to unwind through my workout routine.

"Fine, fine, I'm going," he says, still smiling. Before he leaves, though, he shoots me a wide-eyed look. "I just realized something."

"What?"

"Mom's definitely going to see that article."

My eyes widen as I process that. "Fuck."

"And the plot thickens. Well done, Carlo." Topher laughs as he walks away.

I lean against the wall and let out a sigh. *When did things get so fucking complicated?*

---

CHEERS ERUPT AS SOON as I walk through the doors of our pub.

One of the capos slaps my shoulder. "Well done, boss," he says, grinning.

I shoot him a withering glare and he slinks away. They all slink away when they notice my mood. My jaw is clenched as I beckon Slade over.

"What the fuck is going on?"

He shrugs, rubbing the back of his neck. "I guess they're all just excited about you and the 'Bianchi princess.'"

"And why the hell would they be excited about that?" I ask, walking to my office.

Michael follows. "It's not every day you hear something like this. The story's everywhere. Plus, you're always so cautious and private, Carlo. They're happy for you."

"Hmm," is all I say.

I take a seat at my desk, staring at the documents waiting for me. I gesture at them with my chin, and Michael quickly explains.

"You need to sign off on the warehouse sale tonight. Me and the boys withdrew some cash. We need you to look over it."

My gaze slides over the papers and once I'm done, I offer a short nod.

"Go ahead," I tell him. "And Michael, be careful. "

He offers me a salute. "You got it, boss."

I lean back in my chair as he exits the office. But then he returns five minutes later.

"What's up?" I question.

"There was an issue earlier today in one of the playrooms."

"Playroom" is code for the rooms where our VIP clients get to perform all sorts of unseemly activities at our discretion.

"What happened?"

"Someone snuck a camera inside."

I get to my feet, my jaw tightening. "Who?"

"A part-timer we hired recently. His name's Ricky, 24 years old. He was serving drinks in the room, and the camera was on his shirt. Luckily, one of the capos caught it."

"Does Christian know about it?"

"Nah. The Don hasn't come in today."

"Alright. We'll handle it discreetly. What does the VIP have to say about the situation?"

"He's letting us handle it. I think Ricky was trying to get dirt on the VIP, probably hired by someone. We're holding him right now but he's refusing to talk."

A wry smile touches my lips. "I'll handle it," I tell

Michael. "You work on making sure that warehouse deal goes smoothly."

"Got it, boss."

Something sings in my chest as I head to the room Ricky's being held in. Like my father said, there should be moderation in all things, including beating people up. He never taught me the art of torture, though. I learned all that all my own.

Plus, I really need the distraction right now. Anything to keep me from picking up the phone and texting Astoria. Especially when I have no fucking clue what to say to her.

# CHAPTER 15

*Tori*

N ora was right. I am sexually frustrated. Add that
to the overall frustration I've been feeling these
past few days and I find that I'm in need of some
kind of release. I lean against the headboard of the bed, trying
to ignore the persistent throbbing ache in my core. But it
doesn't go away.

I finally cave in and slide my hand down to my leg. My
mouth parts in a silent gasp when my fingers brush against
my clit. One touch ignites all the pent-up feelings inside me,
and now all that matters is chasing some form of satisfaction
and relief. I lift up the shirt I'm wearing to play with my
breast as the other hand starts to lightly massage my clit.

Sparks of pleasure race through my body, soft whimpers
echoing in the room. As always, a series of images unfold in
my mind. Me, facedown on a bed, ass up while someone
imaginary smacks it repeatedly until it's raw. Then he's
pushing in, setting a hard, relentless rhythm that wrenches
repeated moans from deep within me.

Wetness soaks my fingers as I continue to stroke my clit.
Then I thrust inside of me with one finger, just as the images

in my mind are distorted. I feel the beginnings of my orgasm about to take root when the man's face comes into focus. I hear his whispers in my ear, see his dark brown eyes take in my naked skin. I feel the brush of his lips against mine and the way he fills me so well over and over again.

And then I'm coming; pressure explodes inside me, my orgasm nearly pulling me under. I fall asleep and of course, I dream of him. Carlo's like a drug. And I think I'm slowly getting addicted.

---

NORA GETS a jump scare when she turns on the lights in her apartment the next morning to find me on her couch. I'm curled up in a blanket, my eyes shut tight, but I'm not asleep. I woke up an hour or two ago and came out here to think.

"Tori! You scared me."

"Sorry," I mumble. "Good morning."

I get to my feet and yawn softly, taking in my friend standing in the doorway leading to the living room. She's in shorts and a faded dark shirt, sleep lines across her face.

"Good morning. What on earth are you doing here? I gave you a bed, didn't I?"

"Yeah," I say, smiling. "I just woke up early and decided to come out here."

"Okay…"

"Thanks for letting me stay over, Nora." I run my hand through my hair.

I've been staying at her house the last two nights to throw off my parents so they won't wonder why I'm not with Carlo.

"It's fine, sweetie. I'm always here for you if you have a fight with your fake boyfriend."

I sigh softly in response. Nora moves to take a seat beside me.

"So, are you done avoiding the situation?"

"I wasn't avoiding the situation," I say stiffly. "I was coming up with a game plan."

"A game plan," she repeats blandly.

"Yeah. A plan, a way for us to move forward."

"Which is?"

"I'm going to end it," I announce with fake enthusiasm.

Nora shoots me a long sideways glance. "Okay," she says carefully. "How would that work, exactly?"

"Easy. Carlo and I entered into an agreement. And now I'm going to terminate it."

"Are you sure that's a good idea?"

"Yes."

Nora sighs. "Come on, Tori. You're not fooling me. Tell me what's on your mind."

I let out a soft breath. "I'm just done. We started this whole thing because we thought it would be mutually beneficial. And now it seems like it's doing more harm than good. So it's time for it to end."

"Are you sure that's what you want?"

"Not really," I say on a soft sigh. "But I think it's what's best."

"And do you think that's what Carlo wants?"

"I don't know what Carlo wants," I say stiffly.

"Which is why you need to talk to him. The two of you need to have a conversation. You can't just decide to end it like this. Besides, your fake relationship involves more than just you guys. Think about your parents. Your mom will be devastated."

"She'll live," I mutter.

"And Carlo? His family still needs that building, don't they?"

"Yeah, about that… I think I'm going to talk to my dad about it. I'll ask my mom for help, as well. Maybe if we join our efforts, we can convince him to sell the building to the D'Angelos."

"Is that before or after you break up with Carlo?"

I groan softly, tilting my head back. "I have no idea."

Nora rubs my shoulders. "You'll figure it out, Tori."

I love that she's been so supportive about this. And I love that despite how shitty things seem right now, I have someone I can turn to. It's what I've been missing all these years. A true friend.

"I owe you a girls' night out. All expenses on me," I tell her.

She smiles, her green eyes brightening. "I would say you don't need to, but honestly, that sounds like an amazing idea. Now come on, get up. We're going to be late for work."

She drags me off the couch and we get dressed for the day before driving to the hospital in my car. Our plans to watch some movies and chill after a long day of work are unfortunately stalled when I receive a text from my dad asking me to come home.

When I get there, he's seated on a lounge chair in front of the pool at the back of the house. I take a deep breath before walking over and taking a seat on the chair beside him. I might as well bring up the issue of the building now.

"Hey, Daddy. A little late for sunglasses," I say, settling down and getting comfortable.

He tilts the glasses down to look at me. "I'm trying to be trendy, sweetheart. I hear this is all the rage these days."

"I'm sure it's not."

"How would you know? You spend all your time at the hospital," he tosses back.

"Trust me, Daddy. I know."

He hums softly, a light smile playing across his lips.

"So… why'd you ask me to come home tonight?" I question.

"What? Too busy with your boyfriend to spend time with me?"

"No…"

"Your mother's working all night at the bank. They've got some kind of issue and I wanted some company."

"Oh, so I'm Mom's replacement."

"Pretty much."

"Cold, Daddy," I say on a laugh. "So, how's the company?" I ask, deciding it's a safe enough topic to lead in with my request.

"It's alright. The usual—buying buildings, demolishing buildings, selling buildings. I'm thinking of converting one of our buildings into a women's center. Your mom gave me the idea. It could be a place to provide medical or social services. There could be a clinic, a gym, 24-hour help provided for any woman who walks through the door."

"That sounds amazing, Dad," I say, feeling extremely proud.

One thing about my parents is that they look for any means to give back to society. My dad, despite his riches, has always been humble and he taught me to be the same.

"Yeah. It should take off next month. Let me know if you have any input."

"Sure. Also, Dad, I was wondering…" I trail off.

He seems like he's in a good mood, but there's always a chance he could lose his shit. He turns to me, expression expectant.

"Carlo told me about the building his family wanted to buy from you. The one in Bayside," I start. My dad's expression doesn't waver so I continue. "And I was wondering if you had changed your mind about selling it to them."

"Did he put you up to this?"

"No," I immediately dispute. "He has no idea. He only mentioned it to me in passing once and I thought I'd ask you again on his behalf."

"That building's for my future son-in-law, *cara*."

"I know that. But Carlo's my boyfriend. And we're not planning to get married anytime soon—"

"Tell that to your mother."

"Anyway, the D'Angelos need the building now. Waiting seems like such a waste. You know them and you know they'd use it well. I'm sure they'd be willing to meet any price. So could you please, please, just sell it to them?"

He doesn't speak for several seconds. Then he shrugs. "I'll think about it."

My eyes widen. "Really?" I ask excitedly.

"I didn't say I'd sell it to him. I said I'd think about it. There are several things I'd have to consider. That building's a big asset. And it has sentimental value to me."

"I know, Daddy. But I'm sure the D'Angelos will take care of it."

This is going surprisingly well. He's either in a really good mood or he's finally comfortable with my relationship with Carlo.

"You're the best," I tell him, getting to my feet. "I'll be back. I just need to go get changed."

He nods. "You can tell me all about your day when you get back. And Astoria," my dad calls, making me stop. "If things don't work out with D'Angelo, Dante Marino called me a few days ago to tell me he was still interested."

I don't turn to face him but I do grit my teeth. For the love of God.

"Okay, Dad," I say before walking away.

---

THE NEXT DAY AFTER WORK, I head to Carlo's apartment. Thankfully, he's home—I didn't call or text him in advance. But I ring the doorbell and a few seconds later, the door is opened.

"Hey," he says, surprise clear in his expression.

His hair is damp, strands hanging over his eyes in a way that makes him look really fucking attractive. He's wearing black joggers and a black tank, and the sight of his exposed muscled arms causes my mouth to dry. I'm immediately reminded of the dream I had.

I quickly dispel the thoughts before he sees them on my face.

"Hi. Can I come in?"

He gestures for me to enter and I do so. Then the door shuts and there's silence for a few seconds. I look around the living room, taking in his space. This might be the last time I get to come here.

"Astoria," Carlo says, and I turn to face him. "Why'd you come without letting me know in advance?"

"I, um—I..." My jaw tightens. Seriously, one look in his eyes and I'm a blundering mess. "How's Cara?" I blurt for lack of anything better to say.

As soon as the question leaves my lips, I regret it. Especially when I catch sight of the shadow that crosses his face.

"Really? That's why you're here?"

"No. I mean, not really."

He crosses his arms over his chest, the action causing his

muscles to flex. Can he stop being so distracting for one second?

"Come on, *dolcezza,* spit it out. Why are you here?"

My eyes fall shut as I finally say the words. "I'm here to end our fake relationship."

Carlo's eyes darken. "Why?"

"What do you mean, why?"

"You heard me, Astoria. Why? Give me one good reason why we should end this."

A laugh escapes me. "Are you kidding? There are tons of reasons. Let's start with the fucking obvious one. There's another woman. And I can't even say I understand what she is or who she is to you because you won't fucking tell me!" My voice goes up an octave or two. "Which brings me to my next point—you never talk about what's on your mind. You're like ice—solid, unmovable ice—and I want so badly to break through, but it's literally impossible and I'm tired, okay. I'm just tired. I can't do this anymore."

Inside, I'm screaming other reasons I can't voice. The ones I can't say to his face. The fact that I have feelings for him and the fear that he doesn't feel the same way. And I'm terrified that I'll get hurt in the end.

Throughout my outburst, Carlo just stands there and listens. He doesn't twitch, doesn't blink. He just stares at me. I'm uncomfortable under the weight of his gaze.

"So... um, yeah. That's why I think this needs to end."

Finally, he lets out a soft breath. His voice is low when he speaks. "You're right. I am ice. I'm supposed to be ice because it's strong and cold and it keeps everyone out. Because throughout my life, that's the only thing I've been able to be. So tell me why every time I'm with you, I feel myself thaw. I don't know what it is or why, but you make me feel, Astoria. Do you understand that? You make me fucking feel."

My breath hitches. My throat grows dry, and I have no idea what to say. I'm not sure what I'm supposed to say. Carlo steps forward. His hand goes to my neck, titling my face up in the process. My eyes meet his simmering brown ones.

"I don't have feelings for Cara," he says gruffly.

My eyes widen. "You don't?"

"No. Cara and I have known each other for a long time. If I wanted to start something with her, I would have done so. I always go for what I want."

There's a promise in those words, a challenge. And yet a part of me can't help but wonder if he's really sure about what he's saying. I think back to our meeting with Cara at the party and something uneasy tightens in my gut.

Carlo must sense where my mind has gone because his grip on my neck tightens gently. He rubs against the pressure points of my throat.

"I can't break, *dolcezza*," he says softly. "I'm not sure I know how to. But ice melts. It might be a slow and gradual process, but I'll get there."

I let out a breath. "I'll help you."

"I know you will, beautiful."

We stand there for several moments, staring at each other. Then Carlo's eyes briefly flicker closed, and when they open again, they move down to my lips.

"When I kissed you at the party, I did it because I wanted to. Not because of your mom. I didn't realize she was there."

And just like that, the weight in my chest lessens.

"You did?"

He nods.

"Why? Why did you kiss me?"

A tortured expression passes across his face.

"Because kissing you might be the most fucking addicting thing in the world."

And just like that, I forget how to breathe. Carlo robs me of breath. Especially when his lips land on mine in the next second.

There might be a disaster waiting for us on the other end. But maybe disaster's not so bad.

# CHAPTER 16

*Carlo*

E very single thought in my head disappears as I grab Astoria and pull her to me. She latches onto the front of my shirt, clinging to me, and my other hand snakes around her, holding her against my body. The kiss is hard, deep and rough, filled with so much longing I find it impossible to breathe.

Tori lets out a low moan that elicits a groan from deep in my throat. I tighten my hold on her. We're stumbling backward, my hands moving over her, down her back, and up into her hair. She's against the wall and I'm pressing my body into her and it's the best thing I've ever fucking felt.

My mouth moves down her jaw to her neck, nipping at the skin there. Tori lets out a little gasp when I latch onto a sensitive spot right below her ear.

"Oh wow," she moans.

I chuckle softly against her neck. "God's got nothing to do with this, baby."

I kiss her again and she responds, her fingers knotting in my hair, pulling it, letting me know just how much she wants this. We're both breathing heavily when I suddenly pull away, staring at her, memorizing every inch of her perfect face. Tori looks up at me, nervous, and somehow, I know why. She's worried it'll end.

She has no idea. The only thing that could stop me right now is her. My entire body thrums as I gaze down at her. She's still, waiting for me to make a move. I trace a finger from the dip of her throat down between her breasts. They're annoyingly out of reach. I give her a look, trying to communicate silently what I want. When she nods once, I don't waste a second. I reach down for the hem of her shirt, pulling it over her head, leaving her in only a lacy pink bra.

"You have no idea how beautiful you are, *dolcezza*," I say, my voice hoarse.

"Please," she whispers. "I want you, Carlo."

I never knew four words could be so devastating. I want nothing more than to rip off her clothes and take everything she has to give. And yet, I wait.

"How much?"

"What?"

"How much do you want me, Tori?" I ask, saying the words against her hair.

She whimpers softly when I bite the shell of her ear. "I dream about you," she confesses.

"What kind of dreams?"

Her hazel eyes lift to mine. She bites her bottom lip, hesitant.

"Tori," I murmur against her skin, my hand trailing over the swell of her breast. "What am I doing in your dreams?"

"Your fingers. I dreamed of your fingers inside of me," she finally says, her eyes falling shut as the words leave her lips.

My lips curve into a smile. "Oh yeah? How about I make

those dreams a reality? How wet are you, baby?" I reach for the hem of her skirt.

It's easy to lift it up, and my hand moves to her panties. I yank it to the side, the pads of my fingers immediately finding her clit. Tori jerks violently against me.

"Fuck," I groan as I slowly push one finger inside of her.

"Oh, god," Tori gasps.

She shifts to loop both of her arms around my neck, grinding her hips into my hand, rising and falling with each slow pump of my fingers. I groan again, feeling her tighten around me and wishing so badly that it's my cock and not my fingers. I want to sink into her and bury myself to the hilt, but I also need to take things slow. Especially with her. She controls the pace.

I lean forward to kiss her, desperate to taste her again. Tori responds to the kiss, moaning even as my finger continues to thrust into her. She jolts against me, a sharp breath leaving her lips when I add another finger before teasing her clit with my thumb.

"Oh fuck. Carlo, I'm going to come," she moans.

I increase the pace, doing my best to drive her wild. She falls against me as she comes, her mouth open in a silent scream. Her entire body shudders and I hold her through it. I hold her until she stops, until she's looking up at me again, hazel eyes blinking with wonder. She grips my shoulders tightly to the point of pain and still, I don't let go.

Then, before I can hesitate, I reach forward to kiss her forehead. It's a tender action, one that feels all too easy. Especially when it comes to her. Tori responds by tilting her head up and letting me kiss her again. And again, it's addicting and devastating and I don't ever want to stop. I drag my tongue up along hers, carnal, wet, filthy. Tori's legs are shaking. I'm holding her up against the wall with barely any effort.

Her hands snake down to the bottom of my tank and I lean away slightly so she can get it off. But she's not stopping there. She goes for my pants. One touch of the fabric and I'm wrenching her arm away and giving her a look.

"We don't need to," I say firmly. "We don't need to have sex."

Tori's eyes narrow. "Why not?"

"Because…" I say, suddenly feeling terribly inarticulate. I don't know why I'm stopping right now.

"Do you not want to?" Tori asks quietly.

*Oh, fuck.* I take her hand and place it against the bulge in my pants.

"Does this feel like I don't want to?" I ask her, almost harshly.

"No," she replies. "It feels good, though. So good."

She strokes me through the material of my pants. Tensions racks my body and Tori makes it worse when she reaches inside to pull my cock out. Her hands move over my length, once, twice. It's torture. The best form of torture. She gathers some of the moisture leaking at the tip, using it to guide her movements as her hands move over me.

"I dreamed that you fucked me," she says breathlessly, much bolder than she was earlier. "I want you to fuck me, right here against the wall."

A fire lights up inside of me. I look into her eyes, shining with lust and desire. There's no way I could ever say no to that. "Your wish is my command."

One moment, we're staring at each other, and the next, I'm letting out a hoarse groan before reaching behind her to unclasp her bra. It falls off and I dive in like a man starved, taking one dark, puckered nipple into my mouth. Tori moans, her nails digging into my arms as I shift my ministrations from one breast to the other. I palm the other one with my hand, teasing it, biting it, holding it up and enjoying the marvelous weight of it.

"Carlo," she moans. It's a plea. I can feel how much she wants me. I'm practically vibrating from the intensity of my need as well.

I push my pants down to the floor and step out of them before reaching for her panties. I pull the material until it rips, earning me a gasp from Tori just before I surge into her with one thrust. My mouth drops open as soon as I'm inside her. She lets out a soft cry, her body tensing and tightening. I bury my face in her hair for a moment, unmoving, feeling fire surge up my bones.

She feels... fuck. I never could have imagined she would feel this way. Then I remember something and I pull out.

"Shit. Tori, condom," I say, my heart racing in my chest.

Her grip tightens on my arm. "I'm on birth control. Just fuck me, please."

My eyes flutter closed as I take in her words. It feels like a bad idea, but there's been a lot of those flowing about recently. "Fuck, I love it when you beg me."

"Carlo!"

I chuckle softly, fisting my cock as I slowly guide it toward her entrance. We're both holding our breaths, watching as I slide into her. She's so wet my cock barely meets any resistance and then I'm inside her again and it's the fucking best thing ever. We release simultaneous sighs of pleasure.

"Holy shit," Tori moans. She closes her eyes and I reach for her ass, smacking it once.

"Keep your eyes open and on me when I fuck you. Alright?"

She nods once, eyes wide as I set the pace. Sliding inside her, then out, giving her slow, shallow strokes, designed to drive us both wild. Tori's hands roam everywhere—my chest, my arms, and she snakes her fingers into my hair, gripping it, holding it tight.

"You're taking me so good, baby," I say softly as I shove myself back inside her. "You want to come again?"

She makes a weak noise, her eyes gripping me hard.

"I'm going to need you to be more vocal with that reply, sweetheart," I say, my voice smooth like silk as I slide in and out of her.

"Y-yes," she whimpers. "Yes, please."

I don't miss a beat. My slow pace is gone and she takes it all, absorbing the force of my furious thrusts. Pleasure burns bright inside of me. I grunt softly as I fuck her, about to be taken over the edge. I reach for Tori's clit, massaging lightly.

"Come for me, baby," I whisper against her ear.

My words are a detonator. She explodes around me, her pussy gripping my cock like a vise as she comes with my name on her lips. I have to slow down a little, holding her up as I continue to ram into her, chasing my own release.

I come with a soft groan. Every bone in my body lique-fies. It's a good thing we're against a wall or I wouldn't have been able to hold us both up. Tori holds my body to hers. We're both breathing heavily, sweat gliding across our bodies. I rest my forehead against hers, my eyes closed as I try to make sense of what just happened.

It was mind-blowing. Fucking amazing mind-blowing sex.

"Carlo?" Tori whispers after an eternity has passed.

"Yes, sweetheart?" I say, leaning away and brushing her hair from her forehead.

"Whenever you're recovered, I think I want to do that again."

My mouth widens into a grin and I smack her ass softly.

"I'm still inside you and you already want me to fuck you again? Never knew you were such a good little slut, Bianchi."

She looks up at me, chin raised confidently, a spark in her hazel eyes. "Now you know."

I laugh before finally sliding out of her. Feeling some of my strength return, I lift her into my arms, earning me a soft gasp. She slaps my arm.

"Hey!"

"We're just going to the bedroom, baby. I might as well make good on your request."

I just had her and I already want her again. It's insane. An hour later, we're both lying on my bed, spineless, breathless, and completely sated. Tori smiles softly, moving to kiss my cheek.

"I need to shower," she tells me.

"Want me to join you?" I smirk.

"No." She shakes her head. "You're tired and I'm sore."

A feeling of immense satisfaction fills me as I watch her practically wobble over to the bathroom. She disappears inside, leaving me alone. I stare up at the ceiling, my thoughts in complete disarray. I can't make sense of anything other than how amazing that was.

When Tori returns, she's wearing one of the white bathrobes I keep inside the bathroom. I frown at the loss of the view of her naked body.

"Take that off."

"No." She smiles. "I'm not going to bed naked."

"Why not?"

She shrugs. "Because I'm not comfortable." She pads over to my closet and pulls out one of my black shirts. "I can wear this, right?"

I nod and I'm treated to the sight of her bare ass once more before my shirt covers it up. I get to palm her ass again when she climbs back into bed so it's not so bad. We're silent for a few seconds until Tori speaks up.

"That was…" She trails off.

Her head is on my chest. I don't even have to see her face to know she's biting her bottom lip.

"There are no words, *dolcezza*," I say, sighing softly.

She bobs her head in agreement. "You're probably exhausted. You should sleep."

"If only I could sleep on command," I muse.

"Why? Do you have trouble sleeping?" she asks curiously.

"Not exactly. My body's just wired to go to bed at a particular time. I wake up at a particular time as well."

"You know it's because you're so rigid, right? Seriously, you need to chill out."

I smack her ass for the comment, which earns me a yelp. She lifts her head to glare at me and I offer a cocky grin.

"Just talk to me. It might help me fall asleep faster," I say.

She nods and leans her head back down on my chest. "What do you want me to talk about?"

I ponder that for a few seconds. "I've never asked why you became a doctor. Especially a pediatrician. What made you choose that specialty?"

She hums softly. "I was really sick when I was little. The symptoms started when I was around seven. I had infective endocarditis. It's an infection that damages the heart valves and disrupts the normal flow of blood to the heart. You'd never know it now, but I spent the better part of my childhood moving from one hospital to another. Endocarditis is usually healed through antibiotics, but it took a while before it was detected, and by the time I was taken to the hospital, it had spread. I had acute heart failure and I had to have a couple of surgeries. It was pretty life-threatening. I had surgery to repair my heart and a long recovery time, but I finally started to get better. There weren't any complications after and I'm fine now."

My voice is gruff as I speak. "I had no idea."

"Yeah, my parents kept it pretty low-key," she says softly. "Anyway, growing up like that surrounded by doctors and nurses fighting hard to save my life, I guess it bolstered my interest in pursuing medicine. I'm a survivor and I really wanted to give back in some way."

I rub her arm for comfort.

"One of the doctors who participated in my surgery was this amazing woman, one of the best pediatric surgeons in the world. So, there you go. That's my story, the reason I became a doctor."

I have no idea what to say right now.

She lifts her head to look at me. When she notices my expression, she smiles. "I can't believe I made you speechless."

I swallow softly. "You have no idea how in awe I am of you, Tori Bianchi. You're fucking amazing."

"I know," she says, beaming. She reaches up to place a soft kiss against my lips. "But it really doesn't hurt to hear it."

We fall asleep like that—her telling me stories of her experience as a doctor and me listening quietly, thinking that nothing's ever felt more right than being with her.

There's this niggling doubt taking root inside me, though. Warning bells are starting to sound in my head. Warning me not to get too attached.

After all, I grew up watching my father rip away all the things I got attached to.

# CHAPTER 17

*Tori*

A kiss to the cheek is what wakes me up in the morning, followed by what I can honestly say is the best thing I've ever woken up to—a smiling Carlo D'Angelo.

"Hey," he rumbles in a sleepy, sexy voice that has me tingling.

"Hi," I say softly.

"It's seven a.m. and you need to get ready for work."

He kisses me on the lips. One barely-there kiss and then he's sliding out of bed. I try and fail to hide my disappointment, scowling at his back.

"We can get ready together in the shower," he suggests, turning around to shoot me a flirty wink.

My cheeks heat and my mood brightens.

"Who says I want to?" I challenge teasingly.

He smirks before reaching for me and pulling me to the edge of the bed. "And why wouldn't you want to?"

I shrug. "I don't know. Maybe I'm not in the mood to shower with you."

He starts massaging a spot on the edge of my neck and it

takes a concentrated effort not to moan out loud.

Carlo shoots me a knowing look. "Want me to get you in the mood? I have a few ideas."

There's no mistaking what he plans to do. I grin and nod.

"That might not be a bad idea."

He pretends to think about it for a second. "Lie down, *dolcezza.*"

The tone of his voice sends shivers down my spine and I immediately comply. His eyes are practically gleaming as he stares at me.

"Fucking hell, Tori, you have no idea how you look right now."

He climbs onto the bed, stopping right in front of my legs. I'm only wearing his shirt and my panties, but he doesn't waste a second before getting rid of them. Then he's staring at my pussy. My heart rate quickens.

"So wet already and you said you weren't in the mood," he teases.

"Maybe I'm just not in the mood to have sex with you," I toss back.

His eyes darken. "Make no mistake, darling, this"—I'm not prepared when he thrusts a finger inside me, his thumb teasing my clit, and a moan is ripped from my throat—"is mine. I'm the only one that gets to do this. The only person who gets to fuck you. Understand?"

My head falls back onto the pillow as I resist the urge to moan from all the pleasure. He continues to thrust inside of me while his thumb teases my clit in a rough manner. Then he suddenly stops and I let out a soft groan of disappointment.

"Understand?" Carlo repeats.

"Y-yes," I manage to say.

Carlo grins. "Perfect."

He buries his face between my legs in the next instant, his

tongue going on the offensive as it laves its way across me, then inside me. I helplessly jerk and twitch against him. Carlo places wide, wet, open-mouthed kisses against me and it's the most erotic thing I've ever experienced. The sounds he's making—god! My brain practically goes into overdrive.

My thighs are shaking and breath has abandoned me as I'm overwhelmed with a wave of quivering energy. His tongue dips low, teasing at my entrance before thrusting in.

"Oh, fuck. Carlo!" I cry breathlessly.

I feel him smile against me. My toes start to curl and the pressure inside me explodes when he wrenches his mouth away and his finger slides inside of me. He adds a second finger before his tongue latches onto my clit, and then I'm screaming. My orgasm hits me with full force. I buck and squirm and Carlo holds me as I ride out the waves of pleasure.

When I come back to life, Carlo's staring at me. I blush at the sight of his lips, wet and glistening.

"That certainly got you in the mood, right?" He grins.

My body's entirely boneless and I'm still panting as I say. "You're going to have to carry me into the bathroom."

I make it to work thirty minutes late and unfortunately, I run into Nora as soon as I arrive. I blow out a soft breath.

Damn.

There's a smile on her face as I walk over to her.

"Hey, Nora," I say, aiming for a nonchalant tone.

She arches an eyebrow. "Cut the shit. I know you slept together!"

My mouth drops open. "How can you tell?"

"Are you kidding? You've got that after-sex glow. And you're smiling so hard your cheeks are going to fall off."

I frown. "Can everyone tell?"

"No, I just know because I know you went over to his

place yesterday." She crosses her arms. "So... I'm guessing your plan to end the relationship didn't work out, huh?"

I sigh. "Carlo's very persuasive."

"I can imagine." Nora grins. "Damn, girl. Give me the details!"

"I will, I promise. Later, though. I'm already late. Shatt's going to kill me."

"Alright. But I expect to see you for lunch."

I leave, hurrying for the elevators. Unfortunately, Dr. Shatt has already started rounds when I arrive. I quickly head for my office to put on my coat before rushing to the ward. Thankfully, they're just about to approach the first bed when I arrive. Dr. Shatt raises an eyebrow at my entrance, turning to the second-year resident who's beside him.

"Would you look at that? Bianchi deigned to join us this morning," he says, scowling.

"I am so sorry, sir. There was traffic on the way."

He offers me an unimpressed look. "If you're going to give me an excuse, Bianchi, make it a good one."

"Right," I mumble.

We head for the first bed, "Chart," Shatt says, holding out his hand.

Kelvin, the second-year resident, immediately hands him a file, which he glances through for a minute or two.

"Hi, Calden. How are you feeling today?" he asks the little boy with light blue eyes.

His mother, who's seated by his side, answers. "He said his throat was sore and he's still barely speaking, Doctor."

"Hmm," Shatt says, flipping through the file. "You administered the antibiotics, right?"

He doesn't look at either of us since he's still flipping through the file. But I was put in charge of the kid, so I reply, "Yes sir."

Calden has acute tonsillitis. He was in a lot of pain when he was brought in two days ago and has improved slightly, but he's still pretty weak.

The kid opens his mouth. His voice is dry and raspy when he speaks. "I-it hu-hurt-s."

"I know it does," Shatt says kindly. "But you're a big boy, right?"

Calden nods, his long brown hair falling over his eyes. His mom reaches over to brush it away.

"Good. Have you been eating well?"

His mother opens her mouth to speak but Dr. Shatt beats her to the punch.

"I'm sorry, Mrs. Marn, but I'd prefer it if Calden replied to me. I want to see if he can speak a little better."

She nods, looking at her son expectantly. The kid tells us, with great effort, that he had some soup last night but hasn't had anything this morning. He also manages to inform us that he barely has any appetite.

"Alright, Calden. I'll prescribe you some more drugs. You just need to eat some food and take them. I want you discharged by Friday. Okay?"

He nods and even offers us a smile. We walk away, heading to the next bed where a little girl's asleep. Ashley hit her head really hard while she was playing at the park. She was brought in two days ago with a concussion. She's stable right now but it was rough for her last night. Dr. Shatt asks her parents a few questions and then we moving on. Soon, the rounds end, and I get some moments of respite in my office before I have to head down to the emergency room.

---

"So..." Nora asks expectantly. "Talk to me. How was it?"

I bite into my sandwich, taking the time to chew before replying.

"It was pretty amazing," I say, somewhat sad. "I'm ruined for all other men, Nora. I swear his dick is magical."

She practically cackles when I let out a sigh. "That good, huh?"

I take a sip of my drink, nodding.

"I'm happy for you, girl. I can't believe you went from wanting to end your fake relationship to starting a new one."

That gives me pause. I shift uncomfortably in my seat. "Actually, Carlo and I didn't have that talk," I admit quietly.

"What talk?"

"You know, the talk. About what we are and whatnot."

Nora's blue eyes bulge. "You mean you didn't have a conversation about whether or not you're even in a relationship? Tori, what the hell?"

"It didn't come up," I mutter self-consciously. "When was I supposed to bring it up?"

"I don't know, maybe before bouncing on his dick."

Ouch. I shoot her a glare.

"Sorry. I didn't mean it like that. I just mean, your relationship's already delicate. And now you've added sex to it all without knowing where you actually stand. There's still the other girl, as well."

"He said he doesn't have feelings for her," I say defensively.

"And you believe him?" Nora asks, her voice gentle.

I sigh, leaning back in my chair and dropping my burger onto the plate. I suddenly have no appetite. "I think I do. I don't know, okay? It's all very confusing."

"Which is why the two of you should have talked before having sex."

We did do a lot of talking. It just felt like we were both

skirting around the edges of the conversation. Plus, I'm really worried. Like Nora said, our relationship is fragile. What if I push too hard? I don't want to damage what we have.

I sit up, clearing my throat. "I trust him. If he says he doesn't have feelings for her, I believe him."

"Alright, fine. The other woman aside, you still need to clearly define your relationship. What does he want from you? Does he want you to be his girlfriend? Do you want to be his girlfriend? Are you even ready for a serious relationship, Tori? Because last time I checked, the reason you fought so hard against the arranged marriage with Dante Marino was because you didn't want to be saddled with a relationship."

I chew my bottom lip, turning over Nora's words in my head. Finally, I come to a decision.

"I think... I'm just going to take things slow and see where it goes."

Nora stares at me, her expression studious. "You think that's a good idea?"

"I'm sure that's what Carlo wants, too. I can just enjoy this. It's not often I get to just enjoy myself. We don't have to overcomplicate things."

Carlo's not a sunshine-and-flowers kind of guy. He's hard, jagged lines and ice. He's finally letting me see the parts of him he keeps hidden, and I'm not about to push too hard and push him away.

Nora looks like she wants to argue but she doesn't. She simply shakes her head. "Alright, then. I really hope you know what you're doing, babe."

I absolutely do not.

We go back to eating our lunch but I'm distracted when my phone lights up with a text. I'm sure my face lights up when I notice it's from Carlo. I don't miss the way Nora's eyes narrow, but she wisely keeps her comments to herself as I pick up the phone.

Carlo: Hey.

Me: Hey back.

Carlo: How's work going?

Me: Fine. Although I was scolded this morning thanks to you. You made me late.

Carlo: I'm pretty sure it was a team effort, beautiful.

Butterflies erupt in my stomach and a wide grin spreads across my face.

Me: Whatever you say. So, what's up?

Carlo: I was just wondering if you were coming over tonight.

Me: That depends. Do you want me to come over?

Carlo: Not really.

I deflate like a bubble. I swear it feels like someone took a needle and stuck it in me. I manage to text back a reply.

Me: Oh, okay.

Carlo: No, Tori. Shit, I didn't mean it like that.

Me: You literally said you don't want me to spend the night at your place. It's fine, Carlo. Message received.

Carlo: There was no fucking message, woman. It's just I'm in a bad way right now.

My eyebrows furrow in confusion.

Me: What on earth are you talking about?

Carlo: There was an altercation at the pub and I had to get involved. Safe to say, I'm not in the best state.

My emotions quickly shift to worry.

Me: Why? Are you hurt? I can come meet you. Where are you?

Carlo: No. It's fine. You don't need to leave work. Some bastards got the jump on me and I got a few punches to the face is all.

I gasp.

Me: You could have a concussion, that sounds serious!

Carlo: Tori, I promise this is not the first time something like this has happened. I'll live. But my face is not pretty right now.

Me: That's why you don't want me coming over.

Carlo: Yeah. I'll see you tomorrow.

> Me: No. I'm coming over.

Carlo: Tori...

> Me: Don't Tori me. I'm coming over after work to see the extent of the damage myself.

A minute or two passes before he sends a reply.

Carlo: Please bring some ibuprofen when you come.

Something in my heart lurches. What if he's really hurt? He could very well be downplaying the extent of his injuries. I resolve not to panic and to keep it cool until I can see him.

I get through the rest of the day with him at the forefront of my mind. As soon as I clock off work, I head down to my car and drive to his place. I had planned to go home to change and pack some clothes, but I can wear his clothes tonight and get home early tomorrow morning.

It takes a while for Carlo to answer the door when I ring the doorbell, and I have to stifle a gasp when I take a look at his face. Objectively, I know it's not that bad. He has one black eye and a bruise on the side of his face. Minimal injuries. And yet, something tugs my heart at the sight.

"What happened to you?"

He smiles softly. "I told you. I got into a fight."

"And is that something to be proud of?" I snap, a little angry that he got hurt.

Carlo's expression darkens. "It's a job hazard, Tori. Sometimes I get hurt. I think you've forgotten my work isn't a fucking picnic."

I shut my eyes and rub my forehead. This isn't what I wanted. I really don't want to fight with him right now.

"You're right, I'm sorry. Let me just take a look at you."

We both walk into the house. He takes a seat on the couch while I drop the bag in my hand onto the table. Carlo eyes me and the bag warily as I stand in front of him.

"What's in the bag?"

I reach gingerly for the bruise on his face and he winces lightly. "Sorry," I whisper.

I turn to the bag, opening it and bringing out some gauze, ointment, drugs, and other stuff. When I turn back to Carlo, he's staring at it all wide-eyed.

"What the hell is all that? I asked for ibuprofen, *dolcezza*, not the whole damn hospital."

I smile. "I didn't know the extent of your injuries. Plus, I'm a doctor. What did you expect?"

He grumbles something under his breath that I can't discern. I get to work on cleaning the area around his bruise before applying some ointment, and he barely flinches from the pain. Once I'm done, I pull out some drugs.

"Have you had dinner?"

He nods once, staring at the pills in my hand. "What are those?"

"It's the ibuprofen you asked for, and acetaminophen. It's pain medication."

"Is that really necessary?" Carlo drawls.

"Your head hurts, right?"

"A little."

"Then you're using it. Come on."

I hand him two pills before heading to the kitchen to grab a cup of water. He obediently swallows the pills, drinking some water to wash it all down. I collect the cup and set it on the table before my eyes roam over his face once again.

"You know, you look hot as hell right now." He smirks.

I roll my eyes. "You need to lie down."

158

"I had other things in mind, actually," he says with a flirty smile.

"Those 'other things' aren't happening. You need to rest."

He groans softly. "Come on, Tori."

I shake my head. "No. Doctor's orders. You're going to get some sleep, okay?"

He sighs, getting to his feet. "You're going to sleep beside me though, right?"

Something grips my chest painfully, and I stare up at him. "Of course."

He takes my hand and I let him lead me into the bedroom. We fall asleep together. I know I told Nora that whatever's going on between the both of us doesn't have to be serious, but it feels really fucking serious right now.

# CHAPTER 18

*Carlo*

The other side of the bed feels cold. It takes me a moment or two to realize it's because Tori's not here anymore. My eyes open and I sit up, rubbing my head and groaning softly.

A glance at the clock beside me tells me it's 7 a.m., which means I slept in. Or, at least, I didn't wake when Tori got up. It's odd—usually, I'm a very light sleeper.

I climb off the bed, padding across the heated floors of my room. Instead of going in search of Tori first, I head into the bathroom. I take a look at my face in the mirror. The swelling in my eye has gone down significantly and even the bruise looks better. It makes me appreciate whatever the hell Tori used.

I quickly freshen up before heading outside my bedroom, which is when I hear soft music. I trace the music to the source and it's Tori. She's singing softly while cooking in the kitchen.

She doesn't notice me immediately, so I lean against the doorway, staring at her, watching her face screw in concentration as she cooks. It's adorable. My gawking comes to an end, however, when she lifts her head and sees me. She jumps in surprise, her hand going to her chest.

"Carlo!" she yells.

"Hey," I greet, walking into the kitchen until I'm standing in front of her. "Good morning."

She looks up at me with her big hazel eyes, and something in my chest stutters. I think my heart stops. When it starts up again, I'm grabbing her arms and pulling her closer as I crash my lips down onto hers. Tori gasps into my mouth in surprise. But it only lasts a second or two before she starts to respond, kissing me back with as much fervor.

Something clatters onto the floor when I push her back into the island. I barely even hear it, too caught up in the way she tastes and the way she feels. My hand trails down to her backside and I palm her ass before squeezing it tight.

I'm hard as fuck right now and Tori makes it worse when she moans softly into my mouth. Her nails dig in my arm and it's the kind of pain that drives me crazy. Her hips grind into me, in search of some friction, and I'm all too happy to oblige.

"I want you," she breathes against my lips.

I'm lifting her onto the countertop in the next instant. Somehow, I manage to get her panties off and my cock out of my pants so that I'm able to enter her in one thrust. Tori cries out while I groan, holding her to me. I take the time to look at her then, really look at her—her flushed complexion, the way she shudders against me, and I almost start to feel guilty for attacking her like a caveman. I barely gave her any time to breathe.

"Carlo," Tori says through gritted teeth, "if you don't move right now…"

That makes me chuckle. It's obvious she wants this as much as me. I lean down to give her a kiss before slowly pulling out and thrusting in again. Soon, I set a rhythm that has her gripping my arms tightly. There's a haze in my mind as I fuck her over and over again until she suddenly stills against me.

She looks up at me, mouth open in ecstasy as she comes. And it's the fucking best thing ever I've ever seen. I keep chasing after my own release. A few minutes later, I'm following her over the edge. She presses me to her, holding us in place as I recover my senses.

"You know," Tori says softly a few minutes later, "I'm not so sure what your doctor would say about this."

I pull back to look at her face, brushing away some of her dark locks. "I just fucked the brains out of my doctor. She can let up."

She slaps my arm before her eyes suddenly widen. "Oh shit, the pasta."

I shift away as she jumps off the counter, heading to the pot that's currently smoking faintly. Now that the sex haze in my head has cleared, I can smell the burning food. I walk over, standing behind her as we inspect our meal.

"You just had to distract me, didn't you?" she says, whirling around and biting her bottom lip.

She looks genuinely distraught about our ruined food. It almost makes me feel bad. I twirl a strand of her hair around my fingers.

"Sorry, baby," I tell her. "I didn't know you could cook."

"Well, I barely ever do it. But my mom's tried to teach me and I picked up a few things."

That doesn't sound very encouraging. But still, I brave the odds. "It still looks salvageable, actually. I'm sure if we dish it up, it'll be alright."

She nods, moving to grab some plates while I help her in clearing up the area. As it turns out, the food is a long way from alright. And it barely has anything to do with the fact that it's slightly charred. One bite has me reaching for a glass of water, but I wait for her to take a bite of her own. She immediately starts coughing and drinking her own water to wash it all down.

"What the hell?" she says, like she's not the one that cooked it.

I chuckle. "I think you used a little too much salt, *dolcezza*. And spice and the sauce is—"

"That's enough, thank you," she interrupts. Her hazel eyes narrow. "It's your fault."

"Of course," I say grandly, getting to my feet and grabbing both plates. "Come on, I'll make us some bacon and eggs. And Tori, it'll be in both our best interests if you keep your cooking attempts to a minimum."

"Asshole," she mutters.

Her mouth is in a pout when she gets to her feet, shuffling over to help me out. I place my arms on her chin, tilting it up so she's staring me in the eye. "Thank you for trying to cook for me. You're amazing," I tell her.

She beams. "I'll be more amazing when you don't distract me."

"Sure," I tell her before kissing her softly. "Why don't you go shower? By the time you get back, I'll be done."

"Alright."

I slap her ass as she starts to walk away. She narrows her eyes in what I'm sure she thinks is a threatening glare, but all it does is make me smile and feel warm inside. Once she's gone, I focus on finishing breakfast.

"So, I have two things to talk to you about," Tori says from beside me in the car.

I'm driving her to work since I have to do something close to the hospital.

"Oh, yeah? What?" I question, a little distracted.

My mind is on the people I have to meet. They owe us money, and I'm hoping we can resolve it in an orderly fashion without having to resort to violence. I don't think Tori will take kindly to me getting into a fight two days in a row, despite it being business as usual.

"So, I spoke to my dad. About the building you and your brother want to buy."

I look at her sharply. Now she has all my attention. "Continue," I say, my gaze moving back to the steering wheel.

"I told him to sell it to you guys. After all, you need it, and the son-in-law he's keeping it for doesn't actually exist. He said he'd think about it, but knowing my dad, he'll probably do it. I'm sure he'll contact you or Christian soon," she says excitedly.

"Hmm," is all I can manage, my eyes never straying from the road.

"Wait, what? That's all I get."

I glance at her and the put-out expression on her face. "I would have preferred it if you didn't do that, *dolcezza*."

"And why the hell not?"

"Because it's my problem and I would have figured out a way to handle it. You didn't need to butt in."

A part of me realizes this is exactly what I wanted when I first agreed to our fake relationship. But we've come a long way from that, and honestly, getting the building in this manner feels wrong.

"I didn't *butt* in," Tori says icily. "I was helping you. Most people would follow it up with a thank you to show how grateful they are."

"I am grateful," I say appealingly. "But leave me to handle my own issues from now on, Tori."

She doesn't say anything else. She crosses her arms and leans further into her seat.

"What's the other thing?" I question when she continues to be silent. She still doesn't answer. "Come on, Tori. I'm sorry, okay?"

She huffs out a breath before shifting in her seat, "I got a text from Christopher."

"My brother Christopher?" I ask, a foreboding feeling settling over me.

"How many Christophers do you know?"

I chuckle. "You'd be surprised. What did he want?"

"He wanted to invite me to a party tomorrow night. Apparently, he and his wife are throwing it for his wife's best friend and brother-in-law's birthday."

That's not confusing at all. I got it, though.

"They're throwing a party for Jameson?"

"Yeah. And they invited us. Well, actually, he invited me. He told me to drag you along if I could."

I roll my eyes. "You can't because we're not going."

The look Tori shoots my way is cold and menacing. Shit, she can be scary for such a small thing.

"You don't just get to decide. I want to go. Plus, he said it would be a small party."

I scoff. "Trust me, baby, there's no such thing as small when it comes to Topher D'Angelo and parties."

"Be that as it may, we're going."

"No, we're not. I'll be busy, Tori," I say, fumbling for an excuse.

She gives me a look that says she's not buying my bullshit.

"I seriously don't want to go."

"We're going," she says, deciding for both of us despite what she just said a few minutes ago. "Please," she adds.

When I look at her, I catch her soft expression and the pleading in her eyes. Like I could say no to that. I sigh. "Fine. We're going."

Her effect on me seriously needs to be studied. I swear it's not normal.

Unfortunately for me, Christian and Daniella will not be attending the party. I ask him about it as soon as I arrive at the pub, but he tells me they were able to get out of going because they opted to watch the kids. Then he tries to ask me about Tori, at which point I remove myself from the conversation.

I guess I have no choice but to go to the party. And hope Katherine's able to control her husband's more eccentric tendencies.

---

THE COUPLE GREETS us as soon as we walk into their house. I kiss Katherine on the cheek before giving my brother a quick hug. We're a little late and the party's in full swing. I'm incredibly surprised when I notice the band playing soft jazz music in the corner. It's not loud or boisterous. It's actually pretty tame. I smile, looking at my brother.

"Who's responsible for all this?"

He gestures at his wife. "She and her sister planned the whole thing. We wanted to have a disco ball and strippers but we got vetoed," he says with a pout.

I'm guessing the "we" he's referring to is himself and Jameson.

Topher smiles. "You look happy."

I roll my eyes. "Don't start. I'm going to go get a drink."

Tori's talking to Katherine so I leave her for a bit to get us drinks. Unfortunately, as I'm returning to her, I run into a familiar face. Green eyes, dark eyes and a glare that could melt ice.

"Cara," I say in greeting. "How are you?"

She laughs unkindly. "How am I? Cut the bullshit, Carlo."

I sigh softly. "Listen, I know I owe you an explanation."

"You do." She nods. "And you're giving it to me, right now."

I hesitate. "I could call you and—"

"You owe me at least this much, Carlo," she says sadly.

She's right. I do. I look back at Tori and find her eyes already on me.

I need to talk to her. "It'll only be a few minutes," I mouth, but I'm not sure she's able to make out the words. She nods like she understands, although I do notice her eyes flicker to Cara nervously. She and I head outside to the patio. The cold air billows across my face as I turn to look at the woman beside me.

Cara doesn't waste any time.

"I knew it was going to happen eventually," she says pointedly. "But I thought you actually liked me."

"I do like you, Cara," I say deciding to be honest. "I just didn't like you enough…"

I'm forced to wince at how that sounded. Shit, this is not going well.

Surprisingly, Cara nods like she understands.

"You like her enough, though. Enough to parade her around like she's yours. I wanted that so bad. I still want that," she says softly.

*Ah, fuck.*

If I'm being honest, if Tori and I had started our relationship in a normal fashion, we would have probably ended up here—with me having to break her heart because I just don't see how I could trust anyone enough to give them my heart.

But we didn't. Our relationship's backwards. She snuck inside my heart without me even realizing it and I can't get her out.

Cara was my friend. And we had a really good thing going, but I would have never let it go beyond that. I put up too many walls to allow it. There's no way to explain it to her without making it all worse so I simply say I'm sorry.

"I hate that I hurt you," I tell her.

She nods, hugging her arms around her body. "I'll get over it. "

Sensing that she wants to be alone, I start walking for the door.

"And Carlo," she calls, "I'm happy for you. You actually look human beside her."

I'm not sure what to say to that so I nod and offer her a smile before heading back into the party. I am utterly unprepared for the sight of my girlfriend talking to none other than Dante Marino.

When his hands reaches up to touch her hair gently, rage fills me.

*Fuck that.*

# CHAPTER 19

*Tori*

It's really hard not to feel insecure when a man you're kind of dating is having a private conversation with his former fling. Carlo and Cara disappeared only a minute ago and I'm fighting the urge to go after them. It's ridiculous, though. I've never felt like this before. It's only one conversation, and if I can't trust him, then this relationship isn't heading anywhere.

Katherine excuses herself to go and talk to someone and I'm left standing alone. I'm usually better at socializing at parties and events like this, but I'm on edge. I'm about to head over to the bar to get a drink when Dante Marino appears in front of me.

"Hi, princess," he greets, his familiar smirk in place.

I don't miss the way his eyes travel down my body. Irritation fills me. "Dante, hi. What are you doing here?"

His mouth curves upward. "I'm acquainted with the hosts of the party. And what about you?"

"Same," I mutter, wondering how I can make a quick gateway. I really don't feel comfortable with him.

"Hmm? Only acquainted? I could have sworn I saw you walk in here on the arm of Carlo D'Angelo."

"Of course I did, he's my boyfriend!" I snap.

"Oh, really? So the rumors are true. You're actually dating a D'Angelo."

"Is there a point to this interrogation?"

"Just want to know if you were really that scared of me that you ran into the arms of the first guy who paid you attention."

My jaw tightens. "What the fuck are you talking about?"

He offers me a slimy grin, reaching over to touch my hair. Then he leans down to whisper in my ear. "Don't worry, princess. I'm waiting for you."

I feel a presence behind me just before Dante is shoved back. Hard. I gasp, whirling around to find Carlo, a menacing expression on his face. He doesn't look at me; his eyes are on Dante. He carefully maneuvers me to the side, making sure to place his hand on my waist possessively.

"Stay away from my girl," Carlo states, his voice dangerously low.

I'm torn between swooning because he called me his girl and rolling my eyes because the macho posturing is a little overkill.

Dante continues to smile, an easy expression on his face. "She was almost my girl."

Oh, for the love of god. "Shut the hell up, Marino. Or I'll break your jaw and do it for you."

Dante's not nearly affected enough by the threat. I got to hand it to him, if it was another man, they would have been shaking in their boots. Carlo can be scary when he wants to.

"Yeah, yeah. You D'Angelos sure do like to act like the big bad wolves," Dante says.

"What the hell are you even doing here?"

"None of your business."

"Seeing as this is my brother's house and you just touched my girl without permission, it's my fucking business," Carlo tosses back.

*Without permission?* I almost laugh out loud at that. This is hilariously funny.

Like he was summoned, Carlo's brother sidles up next to him, quickly taking note of the situation. He offers me an apologetic glance.

"I invited him. I didn't realize there'd be friction," Topher says, looking from me to Carlo, to Dante. "Could you please play nice? It's Jameson's party."

He gestures at the birthday boy and his wife as they float around the party, talking to the guests.

"There won't be any problems as long as Marino leaves," Carlo states.

Topher's face falls. "Oh come on, Lo."

"No, get him out of here."

Dante's expression is amused. "There's no need. I'll just talk to the birthday boy for a minute. I was going to leave anyway."

I almost feel bad. He might be a slimy asshole but he doesn't deserve to be kicked out like this.

He shoots me a wink. "See you later, princess." Then he walks away.

Carlo's hand tightens around my waist. Tension is practically vibrating from him. I believe he's one second away from going after Dante. Which would be ridiculous.

Once Topher's sure that the situation has been managed, he walks away. I wrench myself out of Carlo's arms.

"Spit on me next time, would you? It'll mark me as your property better," I say angrily.

He gives me a dark look before taking my wrist and dragging me into an empty hallway. His jaw is clenched tight and his eyes are still bright with anger.

"Do not go near him again. I'm not playing."

"I am qualified to make my own decisions as to whom I can or cannot go near," I say obstinately.

He scowls. "This is not the time to be stubborn."

"But it was time for you to treat me like your toy?"

"You're mine, Astoria. Mine," he says possessively.

"I'm not yours. I'm my own person, Carlo. You can't just lay a claim on me."

Carlo looks like he has reached a breaking point. He takes a step toward me and I automatically take one back. My back hits the wall. I swallow softly as I look up at him. His eyes are gleaming, dark and dangerous. And yet there's a thrum in my lower belly. I clench my thighs.

I lose all train of thought when he wraps his arm around my neck. It's a gentle, almost reverent touch.

"Your lips are so fucking distracting," is all he says before kissing me.

He tastes like vodka and spice. I tilt my head up to give him better access and Carlo responds by thrusting his tongue into my mouth. His hand tightens on my neck while his other hand drifts down to my thigh, drawing me closer. Carlo suddenly pulls away and I moan the loss of his mouth on mine.

He rests his forehead against mine. His hand is still around my neck. It's carnal and possessive at the same time.

"No one touches you but me," he says firmly. "Say it, *dolcezza.*"

My eyes narrow. "You're being ridiculous."

Because despite that passionate, earth-shattering kiss, he still needs to know I am not his possession.

"Say it, Astoria," he repeats, his eyes burning like coals.

"Move, Carlo," is all I say before he removes his hand from my neck and steps back.

"Tori, I'd never harm you."

"I know that," I assure him and he signs in relief. "But I am not your toy."

He walks closer to me and I start stepping back until my back is against the wall.

"I don't want you to be my toy. I want you to be my girl. I want you to be mine. And I don't want anyone touching you but me."

"I don't want anyone touching your lips, I don't want anyone touching that ass.

Then he slides his hand down to my center and begins tracing it with his finger through my dress. "And I definitely don't want anyone to touch my pussy." He softly pulls my chin up to look up at him and slightly bites my lower lip while pressing his hard cock against my now very wet pussy.

"Say it," he commands.

I swallow softly. The pressure in my lower belly increases and I have to clench my thighs. Carlo notices; I catch the dark glint in his eyes.

"No one touches me but you," I whisper, feeling the need to give in.

"Good girl."

His hand snakes downward, lifting my dress. I automatically push it away.

"We're in a hallway!" I say, my voice high-pitched.

He grins, taking my hand and leading me up the stairs to a bedroom.

"Can we even be in here?" I question.

He shoots me a look. "It's my brother's house. This is one of their guest rooms. Get on the bed, Tori."

I would honestly do anything he asks if he continues to

talk to me in that tone. I get on the bed, and it's safe to say we don't make it back down to the party.

---

IT'S GETTING PRETTY LATE into the evening and I'm all alone at Carlo's apartment. We've been together for more than two weeks now. Officially together, or as official as things can get without us actually calling each other boyfriend and girlfriend or having a conversation about it.

I know we're dating, though. He calls me "his" and I spend most nights here. He even gave me a key to his apartment, which is how I was able to let myself in and wait for him. He already told me he might be home late.

I change into shorts before grabbing one of his shirts and putting it on. I have some of my clothes here but I love wearing his shirts which are oversized and incredibly comfortable on me. I manage to entertain myself with a TV show for an hour before I get bored. I would cook us dinner but he gave me strict instructions to "never enter the kitchen without adult supervision." I rolled my eyes hard when he said that.

I pad across the living room and eventually find myself in front of the showcase that's fixed to the wall. I bite my bottom lip as I stare at it, my eyes automatically going to the wooden box.

Nope, I shouldn't.

I avert my eyes and they land on a sports jersey hanging inside a glass casing. There's a number 11 on it and a signature. I had no idea Carlo was even into sports. He never really talks about himself. Something that really needs to change.

Unwittingly, my gaze drifts back to the wooden box. I close my eyes and sigh softly.

Fuck it.

I grab it and, after a moment's hesitation, open it to see what's inside. I gasp as soon as I do so, shutting the box and quickly returning it. After, I wrap my arms around my waist, trying to find some comfort and understand what I saw.

I can't talk to Carlo about it. He'll go ballistic. I need to keep it to myself, at least until he tells me and helps me understand what I saw.

He arrives with Khalil half an hour later, laughing as the two of them walk through the doors. Carlo's eyes find mine immediately. He offers me a dreamy smile and I practically melt. I love how far we've come. His smiles used to be few and far between but now it takes barely any effort at all to draw one from him.

"Hey, baby," he greets, leaning down to kiss me softly on the lips. Khalil lets out a series of coughs and Carlo rolls his eyes. "Shut up, Larsen. How was your day?" he asks me.

"It was fine," I tell him.

He looks back at Khalil, who gives him an expectant look, before speaking to me. "We're just going to have a quick conversation in my study."

"No problem. I was going to work on some research."

He and his friend leave the living room. They return a short time later and we order some Chinese food for dinner. I spend the time getting to know Khalil, who's pretty beguiling, albeit mischievous. He has the aura of a person used to the shadows. Just like Carlo, but Khalil seems more intentional about it.

Later that night, we're lying in bed, and I know I resolved not to bring it up, but I have a problem. When something is bothering me or when there's something on my mind, I simply have to talk it out. No matter how hard I try, I just have to get it off my chest.

Carlo casts me a look. "Whatever you have to say, spit it out, *dolcezza.*"

I sigh softly. My thoughts must be written plainly across my face.

"Okay, fine. Don't get mad…" I start.

"I'll try not to," he replies.

*Fuck.*

"Okay, so I was bored earlier and I ended up at the glass case in the living room. I might have snooped a little and ended up looking at the box."

Carlo's expression darkens slightly. "What box?"

I'm sure he knows exactly I'm talking about, but he's going to make me say it.

"The wooden box. The one you said was your dad's."

"The box I specifically told you not to touch," he says, his voice dangerously low.

"I know you did, and I'm sorry. I was just curious."

"You opened it."

"Yes, I did."

Carlo doesn't say a word. He climbs out of bed, heading for his closet. I jump off the bed as well. He's already putting on a shirt and pants. I stand my ground in front of him.

"No! Yell at me if you're angry, but you're not leaving."

"Astoria," he says through gritted teeth.

"I said no. If this relationship is going to work, you're going to say exactly what's on your mind. Say it!"

He looks at me, dark eyes bright with anger. "What do you want me to fucking say? You saw it, didn't you? You saw what was in there."

My heart clenches and my voice softens. "Who's blood is it?"

He laughs then. A cruel, awful laugh.

"On that bullet? Mine."

I'm taken aback but I do my best to maintain composure. "I thought you said your dad gave that to you? Why did your father have a bullet necklace with your blood on it?"

His countenance softens, and a glint of vulnerability pierces through his tough exterior. "When I was fifteen, I accompanied my father on a business venture. It was meant to be a routine deal, but those other guys got too greedy. The moment we set foot on their turf, all hell broke loose. John Luciano himself shot me, right in the chest."

"Is that the reason your family unleashed a hail of bullets within the sanctum of his private mansion? I remember hearing all about that in the news and thought it was just awful."

"His family, and every last blood relation he had. He had a chance to snuff out my old man and me, and we weren't about to let that slip away without a fight. We went at them with a vengeance, and ever since, our families have been locked in a bitter feud. Well, what's left of them anyway." The way he says it is cold and ruthless.

"Doesn't it eat away at your conscience, taking lives like that?"

He looks me in my eyes and I can see he feels misunderstood.

"Tori, it's not as simple as just taking lives. We don't do it casually. There's always a reason behind it. Our family, we cherish human life, but above all, we value loyalty. That's why my old man gave me that necklace when I turned eighteen. He kept it as a reminder, not to let my guard down. He blamed himself for taking me on that trip when I nearly met my end, but that necklace served as a constant reminder for him. It reminded him to always be the most feared presence in any room, in any situation. So that anyone who even thought about crossing the D'Angelo's would think twice, because we don't play games. If you want a fight, be prepared to wage war."

"If you take a closer look, you'll find another bullet in there, but of course, the blood's been removed."

I consider going to take another look but somehow I know it would make matters worse considering I wasn't supposed to see the first one.

"What's the story behind the second bullet?" I ask, my curiosity warring with my apprehension.

"It's from my first kill. John Luciano," he reveals.

I'm shocked by his confession. "But the news reported he fled the country."

Carlo chuckles. "I remember that. But no, my dad actually kept him hidden until I'd recovered. He told me that if I wasn't willing to exact vengeance on the man who had already taken a shot at me, then I might as well be dead. He handed me a gun, and I took my first shot. Right in his fucking head."

My eyes widen in surprise. I almost can't believe what I just heard. I stare at Carlo, having no idea what the fuck to say to him. He killed someone when he was only fifteen years old? He was a child. Putting a gun into a child's hand is barbaric.

Carlo must see the thought running through my head because he clenches his jaw before shifting me to the side and walking out of the room. I'm disoriented and it takes me a minute or two before I hurry after him.

He's grabbing his car keys in the living room.

"Carlo!" I yell. "It's one a.m., where would you go?"

He doesn't reply. Again, I'm forced to stop him physically by placing my body between him and the door.

"I'm sorry, okay? I shouldn't have looked. It was an invasion of privacy. It's all my fault. Please, please, please, don't leave," I beg.

He looks down at me and his expression flickers for a second before it hardens again.

"I just need to get away for a while. I'll come back in the morning."

"No," I say firmly. "You're not leaving."

"Tori."

He hasn't raised his voice once. His tone is controlled—angry as hell, but controlled.

"I feel awful, okay? I regret looking. Hell, I regret telling you that I looked, but I saw it and I just wanted to know the story behind it. I want to get to know you Carlo. I know what you do and I know there are things I'll never understand but I can't help the way I feel about you. I just wanted so badly to somehow break into that tough exterior so you can let me in."

And now I know and it's honestly morbid. I can't even begin to fathom why his father would do something like that. I never really knew the man, but my parents talk about him like he was a saint. Maybe he was a good person, but I don't know about willingly giving your child a weapon to kill.

"Don't look at me like that!" he snaps.

"How am I looking at you?"

"With pity."

"I'm not pitying you, Carlo. I just—" I falter. "I wish you would talk to me about it. I never would have done that if you'd just tell me about you. About your relationship with your dad. Anytime I try to ask, you change the topic. It's hard, okay? I can't give you a hundred percent and then you give me nothing."

"I never asked you to give me a hundred percent."

I glare at him. "This isn't about what's been asked for. It's about what you give your partner." I pause as I realize something. "Or am I not your partner?"

Something shatters in my chest. Maybe I've been delusional and he doesn't think of me as anything more than a girl he's sleeping with. His toy.

Carlo's expression softens. He looks down at me, his hand lightly grazing my cheek.

"You sleep at my house every night, Tori."

"True, but…"

"You're my girlfriend. My partner. Mine. Okay?" he says, a note of finality in his tone that permits no argument.

I nod. Something loosens in my chest, allowing me to breathe properly.

"Forgive me, please," I say earnestly. "I'll never do something like that again. I promise."

He stares into my eyes for the longest moment before letting out a soft sigh. "I forgive you."

"Talk to me about it," I say, my tone pleading. "You can talk to me. I'll listen."

Carlo's expression becomes pained. "I'm just—" He breathes out. "I'm just not ready, Tori. I don't know how to be ready to just… talk about this shit. I'm Carlo D'Angelo, I don't sit around talking."

I knew. I knew when all this started that he wasn't a man who would open up about his feelings so easily.

"I can wait," I whisper. "However long it takes."

He nods, pulling me into his arms, and I let him hold me. He makes me feel safe, like nothing could hurt me as long as I'm with him. And I want to be that person for him too.

But Carlo has a lot of scars and some of them aren't fully healed yet. Which means I have to give him time to work through it all.

I just wish he'd let me help him.

# CHAPTER 20

## *Carlo*

'm working at one of our casinos when Tori calls to inform me that her dad wants to see me. She's pretty sure it has to do with the building. I make my way over to his company, slightly nervous about meeting up with Salvador. And I'm never nervous.

But Salvador Bianchi's a formidable man, and I'm dating his daughter. I didn't care before because it wasn't real. But now it is. Now that I've got her, there's a possibility I could lose her due to her father, and I'm not about to let that happen.

On my way to his office, I get a text.

Topher: Mom's coming back.

I pull over to the side of the road to reply.

Me: What do you mean coming back?

Topher: I mean she's returning from her trip to Europe, genius. She'll be back in the US in a few days.

I roll my eyes.

> Me: Catzo.

> Topher: She says we're having a family dinner the day after she arrives. And she also said to tell you to bring your girlfriend.

> Me: Fuck.

> Topher: Yep. Good luck, fratello.

I don't dwell too much on my mom's arrival, seeing as I first have to contend with another parent. I'm shown into Salvador's office as soon as I arrive. He gets to his feet from behind his desk, a wide grin on his face.

"Ah. Carlo. Thanks for meeting up with me, son," he says.

I shake his hand and he gestures for me to take a seat.

"How's everything going?" Salvador questions.

"Pretty good, sir."

He arches an eyebrow. "Sir? You're dating my daughter, Carlo. Call me Salvador. We're going to be family soon, we can drop the formalities."

"Alright." I nod, getting comfortable in the chair.

"I heard you were having a problem with Desantos. That old bat just doesn't want to quit, huh?"

"We were having some problems with him but Christian took care of it," I inform him.

"Ah, of course he did. Your brother's a good man. Your father left the family in capable hands. Both of you have been doing well."

"Thank you."

"Which brings me to my next point. I think it's time I finally passed the building over. I was worried in the beginning about you and Astoria, but I can see now my fears were unfounded. I've never seen my daughter so happy. Which is why I'm going to hand the building over. You've earned it. And I'm sure you boys will do well with it."

"Thank you, Salvador," I say, feeling a weight slide off my chest.

At least it's still working out the way we needed it to.

"I'll talk to Christian about coming over so we can negotiate the price and sign the documents."

Salvador waves a hand in the air. "No, no. Didn't you hear what I said, son? I'm handing the building over. This isn't a sale. It's a gift."

I stare at him in surprise. "I don't think that's necessary, Salvador."

"Of course it is. You're my future son-in-law!" He laughs. "I can give you this, at least. Consider it an early wedding gift."

I swallow. Fuck. If he doesn't accept money for the building then I'll feel even worse about the deception that got us here.

"Salvador, just let us pay. It's an expensive property."

"Which is why I'm giving it to you," the man says stubbornly. "Take it, Carlo. Stop being modest. I already had the documents for the transfer prepared. All that's left is for us to sign it."

My hands curl into fists as I debate this in my head. The feeling in my gut tells me that getting the building for free might come back to bite me in the ass. But I take one look at Salvador's earnest expression and inwardly sigh. He's not going to let it go.

"Alright. Thank you very much, Salvador."

At least we're getting the building. There's that. We sign the documents and just like that, my family has gotten something we've needed so desperately all this while. Salvador shakes my hand to close the deal.

"Welcome to the family, son."

"Thank you."

The expression on Christian's face is priceless when I hand him the deed later that day.

"He gave it to you for free?"

"Yep," I reply before collapsing onto the couch in his office.

"That's dangerous. I don't trust free things," Christian mutters.

"My thoughts exactly."

———

AT NIGHT, I'm curled in bed with Tori after telling her the news about the family dinner. She's already nervous and I hate to add to her stress, but I need to talk to her about this as well.

"I think we should tell your parents the truth," I say.

Tori turns around to face me, her brows furrowed. "What are you talking about?"

"I think we should tell the truth about the whole fake relationship. They'll be mad, but they'll get over it eventually."

Tori bites her bottom lip, her expression thoughtful. "I'll tell them," she says carefully. "But not yet. There's no way my dad won't overreact and blow things out of proportion."

I sigh. "Tori, I'm really not comfortable with them not knowing."

She smiles, leaning forward to kiss me on the cheek. "It'll be fine. I promise."

"I really hope so," I say grudgingly.

---

TORI'S A BUNDLE of nerves as I drive us to Christian's house for the family dinner, shifting in her seat and biting her fingernails. I roll my eyes before glancing at her.

"It'll be okay, Tori."

She looks at me sharply. "You don't know that."

"Of course I do. It's my mom. She'll like you. Plus, you're Italian. She always used to say she would love for one of us to marry an Italian."

Unfortunately, that doesn't make her feel better. "I'm the worst sort of Italian girl, Lo. I can't even cook our food."

A laugh escapes me. "Trust me, my mom won't mind about that."

"Just because she can't cook doesn't mean she won't want her son's girlfriend to be able to."

I glance at her again. "How do you know she can't cook?"

"She and my mom used to be friends," she reminds me.

"Oh yeah," I mutter. "Stop stressing. She'll love you. My mom loves everyone."

She finally calms down enough to stop talking until we arrive at the house. I take her hand and lead her inside. Dinner's probably still being prepared by the chef, but most of the family's here. The kids aren't, though, so I'm guessing they're in their playroom.

"Hey, Lo. Astoria," Christian says, nodding at Tori beside me.

She offers him a smile. Greetings are quickly exchanged as Katherine and Daniella move forward to give her a hug. There's an uneasy expression on both their faces. I'm not sure why, but then I catch the look on my mom's face.

She's standing at the doorway leading into the living room. Tori and I walk over to her. I'm not sure I like how she's looking at Tori, but I ignore it in favor of making the introductions.

"Mom, this is Astoria. Astoria, my mother. Martina D'Angelo."

"It's really nice to meet you, Mrs. D'Angelo," Tori says warmly.

I turn to my mom expectantly, waiting for her kind words and overzealous happiness that she gets to meet my girlfriend. Instead, my mom places her hand on her hips, her cool gaze moving from me to Tori. She doesn't say anything for several seconds. I arch an eyebrow at her.

"What about Cara?"

My eyes widen. "*Mamma!*" Is she seriously mentioning Cara now? I'm introducing my girlfriend to her for fuck's sake.

She shrugs, her expression seemingly innocent. "It's just she's the only woman I know you care for. I'm just surprised I'm meeting a new one, is all."

Tori starts to squirm beside me. She was already nervous enough about coming here and my mom's behavior is only going to make her feel worse.

"How do you even know about Cara?" I ask through gritted teeth.

"Topher used to tell me all about the two of you. I was waiting for the day you'd let me meet her," she informs me.

I look at my youngest brother, who seems to be doing his best to sink into his chair and out of sight. I'm sure the expression I shoot his way is nothing short of murderous. He sends me an apologetic look.

"Well, now you're meeting Astoria. My girlfriend. Be nice," I say, trying to keep the edge out of my voice.

Her eyes narrow, which means I failed at that. She gives me her best fuck-off expression, but I stand my ground. This is honestly ridiculous. Why the hell is she treating her like this?

I let out a quick breath. "Mom, can I talk to you privately?"

She nods, walking out of the living room. I squeeze Astoria's arm and offer her what I hope is a reassuring smile, and I give Daniella a look to take care of her while I follow my mom. She's standing at the foot of the steps.

I've never doubted that Martina D'Angelo is a formidable woman, and I've often been a little sympathetic towards anyone who would find themselves on the other end of her distrust or anger. I just never thought it would be directed at a woman I care about, for no fucking reason.

"Why don't you like her?" I ask pointedly.

She looks up at me, "Because I'm not sure this 'relationship' of yours is a good idea. It seems very suspicious."

"What are you even talking about?"

"Topher told me everything. According to him, the two of you started out in a fake relationship in order to fool her parents. And then you started dating for real. How am I to know what's real or not in this situation? You could very well still be fooling everyone!"

I grit my teeth, running my hand through my hair in agitation. "I'm going to kill him," I grumble under my breath.

"You will do no such thing."

Topher's dead. I swear I'll kill him. It's unfortunate that Junior will become fatherless in the process.

I pace in front of my mom, trying to organize my thoughts.

"Why didn't you ask me about it? You could have talked to me instead of letting Topher blab all about my personal life—which he had no right to do, by the way," I state.

"If I talked to you about it, would you have opened up? No. You'd have told me it's nothing and then shut me out. Of all my children, you're the one who talks to me the least. You seek me out the least. You've never seemed to need me, even when you were a child, Carlo."

"That's not true. And even if it is, that's not what's important here," I say.

"You're right. it's not. Your relationship with that woman is."

"That woman," I say, gesturing in the direction we came from, "is my girlfriend, Mom. She's my girlfriend and I care about her. She's a woman I want to spend every second of every day with. I think about her all the time, and I'm pretty sure I'm obsessed. I promise, Mom, our relationship is very real."

She stares at me for an uncomfortably long time before sighing.

"I just want you to be happy, *mia cara*. You're my whole entire heart, you and your brothers. After your father died, I felt so empty. But then your brothers met their wives and they gave me my grandbabies, and my heart was so full, damn near bursting. But there's always been a part of it reserved for you and your happiness."

"I am happy, *Mamma*," I say gruffly. "I'm happy with her."

She moves forward, lifting her hand to my face. "Are you sure she's what you want? No deceptions or lies."

I nod once, my expression serious.

"And she wants you, too?"

"Yeah, she does."

My mom smiles. "Have you been treating her well?"

"I've been trying my best," I say with a smile of my own.

Her smile slips. "Oh. What have I done? She's going to hate me."

"Tori could never. I promise," I assure her. "Don't worry. I'll explain everything."

"No need. I'll do it. I'll apologize and explain myself," she tells me. "I need to start getting to know my future daughter-in-law. And she's Italian. You did so well, *mi amore*."

And just like that, she's giddy.

"That's way into the future. Tori needs to finish her residency before we even consider marriage. She has her board exams next year."

Damn. I have no clue where that came from. She and I have never spoken about marriage before. But I want it. With her. I want everything with her.

Mom grins like she can read my thoughts. "I'm so proud of you, *cara*. And I can't believe you're with a doctor!"

"Yeah, it's fucking crazy."

"And amazing. It's amazing," she says softly. I lean down so she can kiss my cheek. "Oh, and Carlo? You need to tell her parents the truth. You can't keep deceiving them. It's not right."

I sigh softly. "I know, *Mamma.*"

# CHAPTER 21

*Tori*

" I t'll be fine, Tori," Daniella says, rubbing my arms comfortingly.

It will most certainly not be fine. A woman who could very well be my mother-in-law clearly despises me, and I have no idea what to do. I don't even know why. I'm this close to losing my shit right now.

Carlo and his mother return and I launch to my feet. Mrs. D'Angelo smiles at me. It's an uncomfortable, awkward kind of smile. When I look at Carlo, though, all he offers is a quick thumbs up before his eyes roam the room, landing on his brother.

"Topher!" he barks. "Outside, now."

Topher gulps and gets to his feet, doing as his brother asks. I'm a little worried when I catch the murderous expression on Carlo's face. Thankfully, Christian goes with them so I'm sure whatever's going on won't escalate.

Mrs. D'Angelo's still standing by the doorway. She looks at me. "Astoria, dear, I'm very sorry about my actions earlier. Can I speak to you?"

"See, I told you she'd come around," Daniella whispers in my ear.

"You scared us, Martina," Katherine tells her.

Mrs. D'Angelo smiles warmly. She's still waiting for me so I shuffle forward and let her lead me into a hallway. With her standing in front of me, I realize she's really small. She can't be more than five-foot-three, but that doesn't stop her from being intimidating as hell. I can barely look her in the eye.

"I'll apologize again, *cara*. It wasn't my intention to be so rude. I just... I was worried because I heard some unseemly things about your relationship with my son."

"Unseemly?" I question politely.

"Yes. I heard you started out pretending to be in a fake relationship."

*Oh.* Yeah, that makes sense. I can see why her claws came out. I open my mouth to explain, but she cuts me off.

"Carlo has already explained and I trust that the two of you have genuine feelings for each other." She takes my hands in hers. "And so grateful, as well."

I smile, a warm feeling enveloping my chest. "It's no problem, ma'am."

She sighs. "I have to do this with every single one of you girls," she mutters under her breath. "You don't have to call me ma'am. It's Martina, okay? Are we clear?"

"Crystal," I assure her.

She beams. "Look at you. You're so beautiful, and you look so much like your mother."

"Really? Most people say I look like Dad," I muse.

"Nonsense. Salvador's a brute." Martina laughs. "Anyway, I must talk to your parents soon. We'll have a wedding to plan. Carman must be dancing right now wherever he is. It was a secret wish that you would marry one of his boys."

"It was?" I ask, surprised.

I'm not sure how to feel about that. I try not to judge but after all the crazy things I see in the E.R., It's hard not to feel a little angry with a man who put a gun in the hands of a fifteen-year-old boy.

"Carman had his faults," Martina says, and my eyes widen. Is everyone in this family a mind reader or something? "But one thing I'm sure of is that he loved his sons and he wanted the very best for them."

I can't ask her about the bullet necklace in case she has no idea. But there's one other thing I'm really curious about.

"If you don't mind my asking, Mrs. D'Angelo..." She looks at me sharply and I quickly amend my words. "Martina. How did he die? Carlo's father."

There's no way I could ask him. Not after last time.

"Oh, he was in a car accident, sweetheart. He was driving home in the snow. The roads were icy and his car ended up going off the road and he drove into a tree. He was still conscious when he was taken to the hospital and we thought he'd be okay, but there was internal bleeding in his brain. He passed away a few days later."

"That sounds awful," I breathe.

"It was all so sudden. I'm sure Carman hated the way he went out. He probably would have loved to die in the middle of a shootout or something. Not a car accident he had no control over."

"I'm so sorry."

She offers me a warm smile. "You don't have to say sorry, sweetheart. It was a long time ago. I'm better now."

"Still, it can't have been easy. I can't imagine losing Carlo. It would crush me."

Martina's smile widens. "Seeing as you're comparing

losing my husband of more than twenty years to losing your boyfriend, I'm guessing it's pretty serious."

My mouth drops open. "Oh, no. Martina, I didn't mean—"

"It's alright, Astoria. I'm very glad he found his person. If things get hard, you can always come to me. I'll set him straight. He can be pretty headstrong and he never listens to anyone."

I blow out a breath. "Tell me about it."

Martina laughs. "You'll be fine. Just be patient when it comes to him."

"I'm trying to be."

Her brown eyes glide over my face, her expression studious. Her eyes are warm and kind when she speaks again.

"Carman was always so ambitious when he was alive. He never backed down. He adored and doted on all his sons but he employed a much firmer hand with Carlo. Carlo was his first son and Carman wanted to mold him in his own image, I guess. With Christian, he didn't have to try so hard because Christian's exactly like him. But Carlo took a lot more effort." She pats my hand. "I'm telling you this because I have a feeling he hasn't opened up to you about his relationship with his father."

I stare, wide-eyed. Mind readers, I swear.

"He will on his own time. Carlo has a lot of suppressed feelings. I know you'll get them all out eventually."

"I'll do my best."

We're both distracted when we hear footsteps coming down the stairs. We walk out of the hallway and find children that I'm sure are Carlo's nieces and nephew. The boy's the oldest. He looks to be about five or six. He has reddish brown hair and brown eyes very similar to his father's. There's no doubt he's Christian's kid.

He's carrying a child that can't be more than two. Martina quickly moves to take her.

"Easy, Danny. You'll drop her," she says with a warm smile. She turns to me. "Astoria, this is Daniel. He's Christian and Daniella's son."

"Yeah, I figured," I say with a smile. "Nice to meet you."

The kid looks like he's sizing me up. Then he accepts my outstretched hand with a shrug.

"Hello, this is my cousin Christopher, but we all call him Junior," he says, gesturing at the little boy who's practically hiding behind him.

He pokes his head out to look at me before quickly hiding behind his cousin again. I get a glimpse of his beautiful blue eyes and long blonde hair. He's his mom's copy through and through.

"Hi, Junior," I say softly.

Martina takes over, introducing me to the last member of the D'Angelo family.

"This little one's Catherine," she tells me.

Catherine has her mom's red hair and a beautiful toothy grin. She giggles playfully.

"Grandmammy!" she says, her voice high-pitched and adorable. "Who that?"

"Children, this is your aunt Astoria. She's Carlo's girlfriend."

Daniel's eyes widen. "Uncle Carlo has a girlfriend?"

"Yes, he does. Be nice to your new aunt, Junior. Stop hiding behind Dan and meet Astoria."

"Oh no, it's fine," I quickly say. "Take your time, Junior. You can meet me anytime you want," I tell the little boy. He doesn't reply, but I smile. I'm sure he'll grow out of his shyness eventually.

Daniel, on the other hand, is a social butterfly who

quickly latches onto my side as we head into the dining room to have dinner. He's a curious kid and smart, too.

The men reappear as we start to take our seats at the large dining table. I notice Topher rubbing his side. He winces a little as he sits down beside his wife, pulling his son into his arms. Carlo walks over to me, an easy expression on his face, and takes note of Daniel at my side. The kid's telling about his pet frogs.

"Hey, little man," Carlo greets, taking a seat on my other side.

"Uncle Carlo!" he says happily. "I met your girlfriend."

"Yeah, I can see that. You like her?"

Daniel nods eagerly. "She's really pretty. I was just telling her about my frog, Leo."

"Carry on," Carlo says grandly. He leans over to whisper in my ear. "You good?"

I nod. "I am so good."

He grins. I've never seen him smile so much. It's clear he loves his family very much. He's completely at ease around them. When he reaches under the table and intertwines our fingers, I smile at him, my heart bursting at the seams.

Martina said she was under no allusions that Carlo was an easy man to love, but every day, I find myself slipping through already slippery cracks. Cracks that lead me straight to overpowering love for this man.

Dinner is brought out. Martina asks Christian to say grace and then we dig in. Conversation flows and I'm so glad to have been made a part of something so special.

---

CARLO and I are having a movie night. We were originally meant to go out to a theater, but his hatred of being in public is still alive and strong and he convinced me to stay home. He's cooking dinner to make up for it. I'm lying on the couch under a blanket and waiting for him to be done.

My phone starts going off, buzzing incessantly, and I reach for it, wondering what's going on. Carlo walks into the living room a second later. I turn to look at him and see a stony expression on his face.

I frown, putting my phone on silent before getting to my feet. An uneasy feeling settles in my gut. "What's wrong?"

"We have a problem," he replies, handing me his phone.

An article's headline grabs my attention.

"ARRANGED MARRIAGES AMONG THE ELITE: How far will the wealthy go to embrace—or evade—a destined union? The Astoria Bianchi and Carlo D'Angelo faux romance, courtesy of The Metropolitan Gazette."

I gasp, fumbling with my phone, but Carlo's quick reflexes save it. I lock eyes with his intense dark gaze.

"How did they discover it?"

Carlo's jaw tenses. "I'm trying to figure that out."

"But nobody should know about this. Your family would never reveal it. Oh, my God." Another gasp escapes me. "My parents are going to see this."

Worry flickers in Carlo's eyes. "I know. The article broke too quickly for me to stop it. Larsen's usually on top of things like this especially involving my family, but even he didn't know until the article was published."

I take a seat on the couch, breathing out shakily. "My parents are going to lose their shit."

Carlo gets on one knee in front of me. His thumb brushes my cheek. "It'll be fine. I'll take care of it."

I let out a short, bitter laugh. "I really don't think this is a problem you can take care of, Lo."

He frowns and is about to say something else when his phone starts to ring. He gets up and answers the call.

"Khalil, please tell me you know how they found out."

I look up at him, catching the way his posture goes rigid. Whatever Khalil told him must have been surprising. I get to my feet again, moving to stand in front of him.

"What's wrong? Who was it?" I question urgently.

Carlo lets out a sigh, running his hand through his hair. "I'm going to have to call you back, Khalil." He drops his phone and looks at me. "It was Nora, baby. She sold the story to the Met Gazette."

It takes me a second to compute what he's telling me.

"No. No way," I say, shaking my head in disbelief. "She wouldn't."

"Tori," he says gently, reaching for my shoulder.

I shift out of his grasp. "Carlo, she wouldn't!"

He gives me a sympathetic look.

"I can—I can prove it," I say, reaching for my phone. There are about ten missed calls from my parents, but I ignore them and the numerous other texts and notifications to dial Nora's number. It rings and rings but she doesn't pick up. My eyes prick with tears. I call her number again.

"I was just talking to her a few days ago. She sounded so excited when I told her we've been together for a month. She wouldn't... she wouldn't do this."

When I call Nora again and there's still no reply, I fall onto the couch, my body shaking. A sob climbs up my throat. Carlo's there in an instant, pulling me into his lap. He holds me like a baby as I cry.

"I trusted her," I say when I finally stop crying. My voice is hoarse.

Carlo cleans the tears from my cheeks. "I know, baby."

"She was supposed to be my friend."

197

"I know," he says softly.

"Carlo, this is a disaster. What are we going to do?"

"Honestly, *dolcezza*, I'm not sure yet. But I'll figure it out, I promise."

I groan before climbing out of his lap. "I need to go. I need to talk to my parents."

He nods. "Do you want me to come with you?"

"No. I'd better go alone. My dad might kill you if you show up with me before I get a chance to explain," I say. The words feel like a joke but they're not.

Carlo nods, his eyes shuttered and closed off. "I'll get to work on damage control."

He kisses me. "Drive safe, okay?"

I nod and he lets me go. My heart feels like lead as I head over to my parents' house. I don't know if I'm even in the right frame of mind to explain what happened, but I have to do this before they draw too many conclusions on their own.

Carlo and I have come too far for me to let something like this ruin us.

# CHAPTER 22

## *Carlo*

I'm about to lose my shit. I'm pacing from one length of my living room to another, tension coiling in my veins. I haven't seen Tori in two days. Not since she left the night the story broke.

"You're giving me a headache," Khalil groans.

I lift my head to glare at him.

"I agree with Larsen. Sit down, Carlo. Worrying about it won't do you any good," Christian adds.

"You're right. I should just head over to her house and get her."

Christian's quick to shut that down. "No. First off, the Bianchi mansion is well-guarded. Second, I'm pretty sure Salvador's out for your blood so just fall back and let Larsen do his thing."

---

I wake up and there's no one in the room. I sit up, groaning softly and clutching my stomach. I glance at the digital alarm clock on the bedside table and see that it's noon. One look at

199

my phone and I realize I've been unconscious for an entire day. There's an IV in my arm. I rip it out. I'm not in pain anymore and I really need to get my girl.

I'm about to stand when someone bursts into the room. I raise an eyebrow at Khalil.

"How you feeling?" he asks.

"I've been better," I manage to say, feeling a sharp painful prick in my ribs.

I'm pretty sure the fuckers broke one of them.

"We told you not to go to the Bianchi mansion. Did you think you could take down all those fucking guards by yourself?"

"I damn sure tried. I've got to find my girl man."

"I know. That's what I'm here to talk to you about Carlo. We have a problem. Astoria's been abducted," Larsen says to me, his expression tight. "Dante Marino has her."

I swear my heart fucking stops. "What the fuck did you just say?"

"I'm not sure what happened? Salvador contacted my company a few minutes ago, frantic. Apparently, Astoria left the house with Dante two days ago. Salvadore set up the meeting in an attempt to get them to move forward with their original arrangement but it backfired.

They had dinner reservations but never made it to the restaurant. Instead, he took her to some unknown location and then called Salvador, asking him to agree to a business deal if he wants his back."

I silently take all that in. I imagine Dante Marino's face and see red. I'm not thinking straight when I grab the collar of Khalil's shirt, pulling him closer.

"Find her," I say through gritted teeth. "Find her now!"

Khalil rolls his eyes before calmly extracting my hand

from his shirt. He smooths out all the wrinkles before looking at me.

"Don't worry, I'm already on it."

I nod, staring at the wall and trying my fucking hardest not to imagine my girl right now. She's probably scared out of her mind. The only thing I have now is the icy rage in my veins and fear for her.

I entered my living room, finding my loyal crew assembled, awaiting my next command.

"Get Salvador on the line," I order.

The room's atmosphere tenses as I confront her father, "Why didn't you reach out when she vanished?"

"I don't owe you an explanation, Carlo. Not after that charade meant to disgrace my family," he retorts sharply. But then, he takes a deep breath, and his voice carries a note of regret, "I thought I was doing what was best for her. A grave mistake, one that now burdens my daughter."

Frustration surged within me, "She's with me, Salvador. Why would you arrange for her to meet with fucking Dante?"

"You mean that front page worthy performance?"

"It began that way," I admitted, "but now I can't even think without your daughter in my life."

Salvador brushed my words aside, "It's a little too late for an explanation D'Angelo, just find my kid."

Before hanging up, with unwavering determination, I vowed, "I'll find my girl."

Khalil studies me for a moment. "What are you going to do when you find them?"

I look at him then, a cruel smirk touching my lips. "I'm going to make Dante Marino wish he was never born. And then I'm going to kill him."

Nobody touches what's mine.

I took an anatomy course in college out of morbid curiosity. I wanted to learn how the body worked. By that point, I already knew exactly how my life was going to go, so I was always searching for knowledge, always looking for ways to be better at what I was expected to do.

I learned about nerve endings in every single body part. I learned exactly where to shoot and stab without killing a person. I know exactly where to stab to make a grown man feel more pain than he can imagine.

Right now, my knife is buried in Marino's anterior femoral nerve. He just lost all sensory functions to the front and middle part of his thigh. The scream he lets out is practically muted by the time it reaches my eardrums.

"Shut the fuck up. I haven't even started yet," I mutter.

I can't stop seeing it. We were able to track Marino to this hotel thanks to CCTV cameras on the road since we couldn't track his phone. It was a long process and I was damn near out of my mind by the time Khalil finally found him. The hotel's pretty discreet, well hidden. We got inside with barely any effort but had to pay a lot of fucking money so they'd give us his room number.

There was another hiccup at the door. Apparently Marino's been staying here since he arrived in the U.S., and he had enough foresight to install a biometric, password-protected lock. This must be his private room. Thankfully, I had enough foresight to bring along the best hacker I know. Khalil unlocked the door in less than five minutes. Nothing could have prepared me for what was on the other side, though.

I kick the man wailing on the ground before leaning down. "You had my girl tied up like an animal!" I growl.

"I'm sorry," Dante cries. "I'm fucking sorry."

I smile, "No, you're not. But trust me, Marino. By the time I'm done, you'll be more than just fucking sorry."

I look up in time to catch Tori's flinch. Fuck, she can't be in here for this. I give Khalil a look, telling him to get her out of here. He tries to take her arm but she wrenches it away and shakes her head. She stares at me resolutely.

"I'm staying."

Our gazes connect. Several moments pass. I can't tell what she's fucking thinking right now. I can barely think of anything except the way she looked under Marino. If I had been only a few seconds later... I don't even want to imagine it right now. It'll only make me angrier and I'm already so fucking furious I can barely breathe.

I don't have time to convince Astoria to leave, so I turn back to Dante. He's clutching at his thigh, staring at the blood pooling out of it.

"Take off your shirt," I command. "Use it to apply pressure."

He stares at me, uncomprehending.

I cock my head to the side. "Do you want to die?" I ask calmly. He hurriedly shakes his head before doing as I asked. I smile. "Well done. Your arms next."

"It hurts, doesn't it?" I ask, staring at him. "You should have thought things through before going after my girl."

"No!" Tori yells, distracting me. I look up at my girl, feeling something clench in my chest. Fuck. I can't believe I almost lost her. "That's enough."

"No, it's really not," I say, shaking my head.

"Please, don't kill him," she says, her eyes welling up with tears.

I clench my jaw. "Of course I'm going to kill him. He just hasn't suffered enough, and I'd hate for him to bleed out too early."

"Carlo, you have. You've tortured him enough. Look at him."

I grit my teeth. This wasn't what I had in mind for Marino. But I can hear the hysteria in her voice, the way it quivers. She's been through enough. And it's Tori. There's not a lot of things I wouldn't't do for her but letting this fucker live, isnt one of them.

I step back from Marino. He's groaning in pain on the floor.

"Please," he begs but its too late. I'm already in my trance and have tuned out his begging.

I pull my gun out, aiming it at his forehead. "Before I kill you, apologize," I grit out.

"Please don't, I'm sorry!" he cries.

"Not to me. To her."

Dante turns his head to look at Tori. Her hands are clenched tight.

"I'm sorry," he says, tears streaming down his face.

And then, I aim to shoot, but Tori rushes over and stands in front of me, placing a soft hand on my cheek. "Please. Please don't kill him," she begs.

I've never been this close and backed away from a kill, not until now. When Tori touches me, it's as if she awakens something inside me. I can actually hear Marino's screams of pain and his fear. "I have a daughter. I'm sorry. Please, let me try to be a father to her. Please, don't kill me," he pleads.

I still want to kill him, but I can't. Tori's hand on me has brought an unprecedented sense of calm.

"We need to take him to the hospital," she says.

"I'll do no such thing."

"You can't leave him here like this; he'll die!"

"I'm begging you. Please," she cries out.

Reluctantly, I give my guys instructions to drop him off at a hospital.

I let out soft breath before walking toward my girl. Her eyes are wide and fearful. I stop in front of her, wondering if any of the fear is directed at me. But she's not looking at me, she's staring at al the blood pouring out of Dante's body.

"Baby," I call softly. She jerks, looking up at me. "I'm sorry you had to see that."

"Thank you. For coming to rescue me but… Just, please. Take me home."

"I'll take care of things here," Khalil informs me.

"Thanks," I say gratefully.

I honestly don't know what I would have done without him. I step over to Tori and lead her away.

We drive home in silence. As soon as we arrive, she's asking for my phone so she can talk to her parents. There are some tears as she assures them she's fine. Once the call ends, she heads into the bathroom.

I stay in the living room, running my hand through my hair in agitation and wishing I knew what she's thinking right now.

Tori comes back out thirty minutes later. She's showered and changed into one of my shirts. She looks much better and I'm glad. My eyes snake down to the first-aid kit in her hand. She brought it over to the house a few weeks ago. I raise an eyebrow in question.

"I need to change your dressing and check your wounds."

I stare at her for a moment before speaking, "I'd prefer it if you rested. You've had a long day, *dolcezza*."

"Carlo, don't fight me on this."

I sigh softly before sitting down and letting her do her thing.

"Did you go to a hospital?" she questions as she looks at the wrapping around my ribs.

I shake my head. "We have a doctor on call. She patched me up."

"Well, she did a good job," Tori sniffs.

Once she's done checking my wounds, she asks me to order some food so we can eat. She's acting weird and I'm starting to get a little worried. I stare at her warily, waiting for the other shoe to drop. There's no way in hell she has nothing to say about what she witnessed at the hotel.

I clean up the kitchen after our meal. When I return, she's curled up on the couch, staring blankly at the TV screen. I watch her for several seconds. Her dark hair's in a messy bun and her face is devoid of make up, and yet she's the most beautiful thing I've ever set my eyes on. After what happened today, I'm never letting her go again.

Topher once said to me that falling in love feels like getting a carpet pulled out from under your feet. You have no choice but to fall. Gravity pulls you under. No matter how hard you fight it, it's always better to just accept the way you feel. Even if it might hurt.

Falling in love with Tori doesn't hurt, though. Instead of feeling a carpet swept out from under my feet, it feels like free-falling from a cliff and into a body of water. It swallows me whole. I feel it in every heartbeat, every pore, every fiber of my being.

I love her. And I can't lose her. Even though a part of me knows she's trying to pull away. I can feel it.

I walk over to the couch, standing in front of her. She looks up at me, and whatever she sees in my expression has her sitting up.

"You need to talk to me, baby," I say gruffly. "I can't know what you're thinking if you don't talk to me."

"I thought you were a mind reader," she mutters.

My expression doesn't shift. Finally, she sighs, hugging her arms around her body. She pats the space beside her and I sit down, instinctively pulling her to me. Relief racks through my body when she relaxes, placing her head on my chest.

"I want you to tell me about your relationship with your father," Tori says.

I stiffen and she pulls away. Her eyes meet mine.

"You're going to tell me, Lo. Because I saw a man today and he looked like you, but he wasn't really you. I want to know why."

# CHAPTER 23

*Tori*

Carlo doesn't say a word. His Adam's apple bobs as he continues to stare at me.

"Carlo," I say softly.

His eyes flicker shut and he runs a hand through his hair. "It doesn't matter, Tori," he tells me.

I immediately shake my head. "It matters so much. You have no idea how much it matters. To me, to you. So just, please, answer me honestly. I'm begging you."

Dark brown eyes graze over my face. For a moment, I think he's going to brush it off and hide it all away again. Then he opens his mouth, surprising me.

"As you know, I'm my father's first son. First children usually have a lot riding on them, and in my family, it was no different. He had a lot of expectations for me. He wanted me to be the best because I was meant to be his legacy. His successor. Growing up, I had to be the best in school, the biggest, the strongest. He pushed me to exceed all his expectations, and I tried my best but it was never enough. My younger brothers have always been smarter than me. Hell, Topher's a fucking genius." He lets out a wry laugh.

I hold my breath. I don't say a single word because this is what I've needed all this time. For him to open up to me. I just want to know who he really is.

"It was like, I could never really measure up. But what I could do is try my fucking hardest when it came to the family business. When I was younger, I thought I was going to be the next Don. Then my dad placed that gun in my hand when I was fifteen and told me to shoot. Christian had to do the same when he was sixteen. It's kind of a D'Angelo family tradition, except Topher was exempted," he says bitterly.

"After I shot the man, I blacked out. I was so shaken up, I think I might have even repressed the memory for a bit. But after I realized I could block out the screams, it wasn't that bad. My dad told me I needed to be at the top of the food chain or risk getting eaten. Failure was not an option. He made it clear that if anything happened to him, the entire family is my responsibility and I have taken that very seriously. I'm pretty sure my dad decided Christian would be a better successor than me after that night. So, I could remain in the shadows and do whatever's necessary to keep everything together. There were expectations and I needed to live up to them. He would take me along to every job, and every time someone deserved to die, I had to be the one to take their life. I cut off all the friends I had. I even had a girlfriend, but I had to break up with her. Soon enough, there was no going back. I was forced to become exactly what my father wanted me to."

"How could he do that to you?" I ask, my voice trembling.

He looks at me coolly, "Make no mistake, Tori, my father wasn't a good man. But he was a good man to his family, his friends, the people he cared about. He was honorable in the ways that counted but in the world we live in, sometimes you need a ghost. Everything he did to me, every lesson, every action, was taken to make me stronger. He wanted me to be strong enough to take care of my family, and that's what I've done every day since he died."

"No," I say. "Your father made you who you are! I don't know your brothers very well but it seems to me like they made their own choices. They became who they were meant to be while you were forced to become someone you never really were."

Carlo gives me a dull look. "What are you talking about, *dolcezza*?"

"I need you to hear me," I say desperately. "You are much more than the person he made you become."

Carlo gets to his feet. I can tell he's reaching his breaking point. "I've been this person for more than half my life, Tori. This is who I am."

"No. I can't accept that," I say, unable to stop the words flowing past my lips. Carlo's expression doesn't change. He's hiding behind his walls again. "I watched you torture a man almost to death today, and the worst part is, you looked like you enjoyed it."

He looks away. "You knew, Tori. You knew who I was when you became mine."

"You're right, maybe deep down I did. And maybe I could have ignored it, but I saw it. I saw it all today and that's not what I want for myself."

The words come out in a rush. My heart begins to pound because although I've been thinking about it since we left the hotel room, a part of me still can't believe the words I'm saying to him.

Carlo's eyes flicker with hurt. "What's that supposed to mean?"

"Carlo, I'm a doctor. I work to save people's lives. I can't come home to you every day knowing you might have just killed someone in the most brutal way possible."

Tension rolls across his body. His jaw tightens. "He kidnapped you Tori, he could've hurt you. I should've killed that fucker," he says coldly.

I stand and reach up to place my hand on his jaw, forcing eye contact. "I'm telling you now that it doesn't have to be."

He pulls away angrily. "What do you want from me, woman?"

"I want you to stop," I say softly. "I want you to choose me."

He continues to stare at me blankly.

"Walk away from it, Carlo. I want you to walk away from the mafia," I finally say.

He doesn't say anything for several seconds. Then his eyelids flutter shut. When he speaks again, his words are hollow, crushed.

"I can't do that."

"Then I can't be with you," I say, hating with all my heart that I'm giving him an ultimatum.

But I don't have a choice. I can't be with a man who could do something so horrible without a second thought. He has a heart deep within, and I want to help him heal it. But for me to do that, he has to leave all the anger and pain behind.

Carlo doesn't speak after that. I watch as he grabs the keys to his car. After one last look at me, he leaves the apartment. Something shatters in my chest, but I console myself with the knowledge that he has to come back and give me an answer.

I head into our bedroom and climb into the bed. It feels so empty without him, but at least it feels like him. A part of me can't believe I just told him I would leave. Because when it all comes down to it, I'm not so sure I can.

*I love him,* I think to myself, just before I fall asleep.

---

WHEN I OPEN MY EYES, Carlo's standing in the room. He's enshrouded by the darkness, which clings to him in a way that worries me. I look in his eyes, trying to see any inkling of what he's decided, but it's carefully black. I check the digital clock on the side of the bed and it's four a.m.

"Where were you?" I ask quietly.

"I was talking to my brother."

"Which one?"

"Christian," he replies before taking a seat on the bed. I sit up as well, pulling my knees up and resting my head on them as I look at him. There's a lot of space between us. "We had a long conversation. We had some pretty big things to decide."

"And what did you decide?" I ask, my heart thudding in my chest.

He doesn't reply. Instead, he starts talking about something else. "You know you bulldozed into my life? Literally, you crashed into me that day at your parents' party and nothing's ever been the same since. I hate how much it's changed. Life was so easy before. I knew what I wanted and I was content. I might not have been happy, but at least I could live every day without this painful feeling in my chest that I get whenever I look at you."

I suck in a breath. "I'm sorry I hurt you so much."

"Let me finish." He glares. "You want to know what that pain is? I feel it every time I look at you. I feel it every time I see you smile, every look, every breath, every kiss. It's embedded in my heart, the way you make me feel. It drives me fucking insane. You haven't hurt me, Tori. Because that pain, it's a reminder that I'm still alive. You make me feel fucking alive."

He looks at me then, his eyes shining with so much emotion it takes my breath away.

"I once told you that I'm ice and that you were making me thaw. I told you to be patient. Well congratulations, *mi amore*. Because I don't feel like fucking ice anymore. You've shattered me. I've completely melted. You damned us both in the process, though. My heart, my soul, my whole entire being now belongs to you. Because I fucking love you. Do you understand me, Astoria? I love you."

I swear I've stopped breathing. All I can do is stare at Carlo and wonder if those words really came from his lips.

"Would you please say something? I'm losing my mind here," he mutters.

"And what about the... you know, killing." I ask him, my voice tinged with concern.

He meets my eyes and reassures me, "I promise to be more discerning when it comes to that."

I fix him with a skeptical glare. "Alright, let's be clear, a little bit less doesn't cut it," I retort.

He chuckles, "Okay, how about I promise to significantly reduce it? Or I can call you and we can discuss each kill before I pull the trigger?" He suggests.

"What? No. Please don't do that. Why can't you just call the police when things go south, like regular people? Not every transgression deserves a death sentence," I suggest.

He raises an eyebrow, a hint of sarcasm in his tone, "Oh, sure. 'Hey, officer, this guy owes me $20,000 from some illicit dealings over here.' I'm sure that would work."

I can't help but laugh at the absurdity of the idea. "Alright, fine, I see your point. But it's still not good enough."

"Okay, I'll talk to Christian and see if we can outsource our... problem-solving."

My eyes widen, "What?"

He chuckles and places a hand on mine, his tone now earnest, "I'm kidding, love. I'm kidding. I want you to feel safe with me. We'll figure it out, ok?"

"Ok?" he asks again.

I don't speak. Instead, I climb into his lap, careful to avoid his injuries. I wrap my arms around his neck, staring into his eyes.

"I love you too," I whisper, saying the words for the first time.

My heart soars, and when Carlo smiles, it feels like I'm drowning. I kiss him then. Like he's the air I need to survive.

He kisses me back, searing himself into my heart and soul. The next few moments pass with both of us trying to take off our clothes in a rush. Once his shirt comes off, I stare at the bandage across his stomach and suck my bottom lip into my mouth.

"I don't think we should have sex," I say. "You're injured."

"No way in hell you're keeping me from getting inside you," Carlo mumbles as he reaches forward to tweak my nipple.

I laugh, shifting out of the way. "Alright, fine. But first…"

My hands trails down to his hard cock. Before he can stop me, I wrap both palms around his entire length, one fist on top of the other pumping tightly and dragging his skin back and forth. I occasionally flick my thumb across the tip to gather the precum leaking out of it. Carlo's breathing heavily, still as stone. I smile softly before kneeling on the bed.

"Want me to suck you off, baby?" I ask with a teasing smile, my hands still working him up and down.

He jerks a nod, his eyes fluttering shut as I close my mouth over his length. He's too big and it feels intimidating so I settle for slow licks, before trying to take him down my throat. Eventually I'm able to take him to the hilt and I stay there for a minute, with my lips stretched wide against the base of his shaft.

Carlo lets out a low curse as his hands move to tangle in my hair. I settle into a rhythm, licking and sucking until I feel his muscles tighten.

"Fuck, Tori," Carlo groans when I gently suck his head before sliding him all the way down my throat again.

Drool leaks from the corners of my stuffed mouth, sliding down my chin, but I don't stop. I've never liked giving blowjobs, simply because the men I've been with in the past have made it feel like an obligation. But Carlo's never asked for it. And right now, as I'm kneeling in front of him, all I can feel is immense pleasure at the power I'm currently holding over him.

"That's it, baby. Take every single fucking inch. Just like that," Carlo praises.

I take him in again and gag when he thrusts against my throat. Then Carlo stops me. He grabs my arm and yanks me up until I'm in his lap.

"I want to come with my cock in your pussy, *dolcezza*."

I blink at him, still trying to inhale as much air as possible. He wipes some of the moisture from my mouth before ripping off my panties. I groan.

"Carlo, I swear if you tear another one of these…"

"I'll buy you as many as you fucking want as long as you ride me right now. I want to feel your pussy gripping me tight. Just like it was made to."

His words go straight to my pussy and desire pools between my legs. I rise before slowly sinking down on him, gasping softly as I take every inch of him. I stay put for several seconds. We both stare at each other, feeling the mind-blowing pleasure.

Carlo's hands are on my ass. "Move," he orders.

I don't. I shift with him still inside me and he clutches my ass, keeping me in place. I smile at his tortured expression.

"I swear to god, *mi amore*, if you don't fucking move right now."

"Okay, okay," I mutter before rising and then slowly sinking down onto him again.

He lets me set the pace. I feel the bite of his fingers on my ass, pushing me downward with each thrust forward. I squeeze my thighs tight around him, feeling his cock pulsing inside of me. When I slam down on him, a feral look crosses his face and Carlo is clearly done letting me stay in control. His palm clamps against my ass as he powers upward, driving into me, over and over again until I'm a shaky, mindless mess.

His fingers find my clit, stroking and teasing until I go off like a rocket, shaking so hard I can barely stay on top of him. He clasps me against his chest as he continues pounding into me until he's the one shuddering. He comes with a soft gasp.

We both stay unmoving for several minutes, the room quiet except for our pants. When I regain my composure, I lean away and look him in the eye.

"I want to do that forever. I want to be with you forever," I say softly.

Then he says the words I've wanted to hear since I opened my eyes and saw him in the room.

"I choose you, Tori. I'll always choose you," he promises.

A tear slides down my cheek at that. We still have a long

way to go, the two of us. But I have no doubt that he'll be alright in the end. Because I'm his and he's mine. We were made for each other. The minute I crashed into him, our fates were sealed.

And there's no going against fate.

"I love you. So much, Carlo."

He pushes a hand through my hair. "I know, *dolcezza*."

"What are we going to do about our contract?" I question.

He replies with a confident smile, "Don't worry, I'll replace it with another one."

His words fade into the background as his lips meet mine, momentarily causing me to forget all about my **contract with the mafia boss.**

*Carlo*

The church pews are packed with family, friends, and acquaintances. I'm standing at the altar with Topher, Christian, and Khalil at my side, and I'm nervous as hell. I catch my mom's eyes. She's seated at the very front. She gives me an encouraging smile, blowing me a kiss.

Then the music starts and the doors to the church open. My bride glides inside on her father's arm. She looks like a dream come true. When she and her father get there, I stretch out my hand and Salvador places her hand in mine. Then he clutches my shoulder and smiles at me.

We've come a long way. He had his men beat me up, I asked Khalil to help me fuck with his company in revenge, but ultimately, we've settled our differences. All those little things that allowed today to be possible.

I help her up onto the podium, squeezing her hands. She smiles at me, her eyes bright and happy.

"You're the best thing that's ever happened to me, Astoria D'Angelo," I say softly.

She giggles. "Hey, I'm still a Bianchi. It's not over yet."

"You became a D'Angelo the day I fell in love with you," I say. She lets out a soft sigh of agreement.

A part of me almost can't believe we're here. The ceremony starts and somehow I manage to say the right words at the right times. When we need to exchange the rings, Daniel steps forward, holding them in his small hands. He looks good in his tux. He plays his role perfectly and I wink at him as he returns to sit beside his mother.

Tori and I exchange our rings, and the bishop pronounces us husband and wife.

"You may now kiss the bride."

That's all I need to hear. I lift her veil before wrapping my arms around her waist and pulling her to me. She fits against me so well. It's how I know she was made for me. We kiss and cheers erupt in the church. We continue kissing until the cheers turn to whistles and catcalls. Then the bishop clears his throat and we break apart. My heart is racing in my chest.

Tori leans closer to whisper in my ear. "Now I'm an official D'Angelo."

At the reception, we share our first dance and cut the cake, all boring traditional wedding things. All I can think about is having her all to myself, but first we need to get through the sea of family members and well-wishers.

Nora Meccano steps forward at one point, leaning down to hug Astoria. We spoke to her a few days after the events that folded due to her betrayal. She came to us on her own, teary-eyed and apologetic. Tori forgave her, of course. Because my girl has the biggest heart, and sometimes I think she's too good for everyone else.

"Congratulations, Tori. I'm so happy for you," Nora says.

Tori smiles. "Thanks."

"And congratulations, Carlo," she says to me, her expression uneasy.

I simply nod. Nora walks away. Tori slaps my arm as soon as she does so.

"Ow, Mrs. D'Angelo. Keep the violence to a minimum," I say, unable to keep the smile out of my voice.

She rolls her eyes. "Be nice."

"I'm always nice,' I say with a wink.

She huffs out a breath but is quickly distracted when someone calls her name.

Later that night, my brothers pull me over to have a drink. Topher wraps an arm around me.

"I can't believe we're here. I've got to be honest, Lo, a part of me thought you'd die single and alone."

"Nice, Toph. Real nice."

"What he means to say is that we're proud of you, big brother," Christian says, a big smile on his face.

"Yep," Toph says, giving me a thumbs up. "You did well for a black knight."

I roll my eyes. I never would have guessed a few years ago that we'd all be here, happy together with families of our own. But we did it. We made it, and I know for a fact our old man would be happy, wherever he is.

I stand with my brothers for a few more seconds before Tori calls me over. She kisses me softly and I grin. I think I'll be in awe every day that she's mine.

But we chose each other. And we'll continue to do so for the rest of our lives.

"Honey, could you do me a favor and escort me to my seat? I suddenly feel a little lightheaded," Tori requests.

"Lightheaded? Are you alright?" I ask, worry evident in my voice.

She reassures me with a smile, "Yeah, I just haven't eaten anything, and it's messing with me. I'll be fine."

"Alright," I say, holding her hand as we make our way to our table.

As we approach our seats, Tori leans in and whispers in my ear. "I have something to tell you," she says, her eyes sparkling with excitement.

I lean in to hear her better, and she drops the bombshell,

"I'm pregnant."

The END.

**Did you like this book? Then you'll love ...**

**Forbidden Bond**
**An Enemies to Lovers Mafia Romance**

**Hating him was easy.**
**Working for him was complicated.**
**Getting pregnant by the mafia heir... is forbidden.**

I was stranded and the hot millionaire came to my rescue.

His cocky demeanor practically dared me to reject his offer but, I figured it was only one ride and I would never see him again, right? Wrong!

Weeks later, I walked into my new job, and there he was sitting at my boss's desk.

One day, I went into his dimly lit office to find him shirtless.
My traitorous eyes flickered down to his lips,
every inch of me begging to close the gap and he gladly obliged.

There's only one problem.

My boss's family runs the mafia and mine, runs the FBI.
Our families have made it clear that our love defies every rule

and is strictly forbidden.

Read: FORBIDDEN BOND now
https://www.amazon.com/dp/B0CJ4R94W7

Printed in Great Britain
by Amazon